LORELESS

....

P J WHITTLESEA

Tyet Books
Amsterdam, The Netherlands

Published by Tyet Books, Amsterdam
www.tyetbooks.com
information@tyetbooks.com

Structural Editing: Nicole Bauritius
Cover Art: Monique Wijbrands

Ordering Information:
Quantity sales. Special discounts are available on quantity purchases by corporations, associations, and others. For details, contact the "Special Sales Department" at the address above.

Loreless/ P J Whittlesea. -- 1st ed.
ISBN 978-94-92523-00-6

Many thanks to the people of the Wallace Rockhole Aboriginal Community for their inspiration and generosity.

For Robert, Sabine and Mirjam

The coming of the white man was in itself a blessing. We were isolated from the world's culture. It is true that my people could not adapt themselves to civilization, but that is because it came too suddenly for us.

–DAVID UNIAPON, 1925

ONE

···

THE ROADHOUSE

THE BUS

The Greyhound bus jolted to a halt and woke Billy from his alcohol-induced stupor. Through the haze and as if underwater, he could hear indistinct voices. He fought to gain control over his clouded mind. As he did the voices began to recede into the distance. He opened his eyes and forced them into focus. In the semi-darkness and about half a metre from his nose was a cotton and plastic wall with a garish pattern. It was the rear of a steeply reclined bus seat. He tried moving but realised he couldn't. Curled up in a tight ball, he was jammed between the aisle armrest and the side of the bus. Totally soaked in sweat, his right cheek was firmly stuck to the vinyl seat. With some difficulty he pried it loose, making a loud, ripping sound in the process. He cringed. Rubbing his cheek, he gripped the headrest of the seat in front and dragged himself into an upright position. He attempted to peer out of the window. It was dripping wet with condensation from the air conditioning. With limited success he wiped it partially dry with the sleeve of his jacket. Looking through the moisture-smeared window he could just make out some fuel bowsers and the facade of a roadhouse. Everything was bathed in a bright, urine-tinged light.

Billy untangled himself. He stretched out his long, thin legs, clambered out from between the seats and stood up unsteadily in the narrow aisle. The rest of the vehicle was completely deserted. Fixing his sights on the windscreen at the front of the bus he lurched forward down the mild incline. Half jogging and flatfooted, he barely managed to avoid falling headlong down the curved stairs leading to the exit. He saved himself at the last minute by desperately grabbing the door frame. Gingerly he lowered himself down the last high step. He let out a slight sigh as he felt the comfort of terra firma solidly refusing to give way beneath his sneakers.

Steadying himself on the open bus door he scanned his surroundings. The roadhouse and fuel pumps were well lit by several large floodlights, all of which were attracting a huge variety of insect life and were heavily festooned with spider webs. The bus itself stood on the circumference of the light, about ten metres from the roadhouse. Everything outside the reach of the lights was pitch black. He could make out the interior of the roadhouse and noted a few patrons sitting around tables. The reek of week-old cooking fat swept under his nostrils and he felt the bile rising in his throat. He spied a half-open door on the side of the building. The silhouetted figure of a gentleman in evening dress was placarded above the entrance. Billy held his breath, took careful aim at this newly acquired target and stumbled across uneven concrete to the door.

Inside, a filthy basin coated in a fine layer of red dust jutted out from the wall. It was starkly illuminated beneath a single, flickering, fluorescent tube. To his left was a cubicle with a seatless toilet bowl. His eyes quickly snapped from one to the other. He chose the latter. He slammed one hand against the wall, leant over the toilet and puked up the contents of his stomach with a grunt. His head started throbbing. Stumbling out of the cubicle, he lunged towards the basin, caught himself and turned on the tap. There was a distant creaking sound, and thick, brown water gushed out before turning somewhat clearer a few moments later. He cupped his hands under the torrent and splashed water onto his face. He repeated this several times before taking a large mouthful. The water had a distinct, metallic taste. His vision, which had been somewhat nebulous up to now, began to sharpen. His head, however, was still thumping like a street percussionist with no sense of rhythm.

Billy assessed his own features in the rusty mirror above the basin. He was in his mid twenties, of medium build, his skin having a slight brown hue, although his recent exertion had lent it a definite red tinge. His prominent nose was flat and spread broadly across his face. His hair was jet black with loose curls, which many a woman would have relished. It was difficult to determine his ancestry and at first glance you might presume he was of Indian or Pakistani descent. Billy gazed into his bloodshot eyes. Under healthier circumstances his right eye would have been a deep brown. His left eye was an odd mix of blue and green. He surveyed his creased shirt and, pleased that he hadn't soiled it, made a futile attempt to smooth it flat.

Billy's eyes dropped to the gold chain around his neck, and a number of events over the past twenty-four hours began to drift into his consciousness. Not all of them were clear but one thing was: he had no idea where he was right now. Not wearing a watch, he also had no idea what time it was, or even which day. He knew that the chain signified his recent engagement to his girlfriend and that they had plans to marry soon. He feared that he would miss, or had already missed, that most important of appointments. The ceremony was scheduled for the day after his buck's party. The party itself had begun in the early afternoon, and he had spent it in the beer garden of his local pub with his friends, a group of ex-university students. They were all prone to consuming vast amounts of alcohol and also adept at planning boyish pranks. After spending several hours in the sun, combined with the alcohol, he had begun to feel decidedly unwell. Eventually, all ability to maintain clear vision deserted him. In the early evening his friends had offered to arrange to get him safely to bed and convinced him that he could sleep it off on the trip. He vaguely remembered them putting him in what he thought was the back seat of a taxi; now it was obvious the vehicle was quite a bit larger, and that there was more than one back seat. He had then drifted off into a comatose state, and that was the last thing he could recall.

How his mates had managed to sneak him onto a bus was beyond him, but he knew they were capable of all sorts of miracles. In his university days he had once woken to find himself with his hands taped together, his body bound with rope to his mattress and in the centre of somebody's dorm room where a wild party was in full swing. He had vivid memories of a very drunken woman attempting to release him with a pair of scissors. Much to his distress, and being incapable of defending himself, he recalled the mortal fear he felt that she would sever more than just the rope. Later that night his friends had transported him, mattress and all, back to his own room. They had generously stopped on the way to tilt the mattress to one side and stick his head in a bucket, enabling him to perform what was commonly known, in college terms, as a technicolour yawn. It was clear that yet again he had been the victim of his own inability to curb his alcohol intake. It also slowly dawning on him that, unfortunately, this time a rescue party would not miraculously arrive to steer him back to the safety of his own bed.

Billy shook his head violently and splashed more water in his face. It was time for decisive action. Clenching the basin firmly with both hands he stared intensely once more at his own visage, before doing a deft about-turn and stepping out into the darkness. He heard the driver gunning the bus's engine. In panic he sprinted towards the road. Before he had reached it all that remained of the bus were its taillights dimming in the distance.

'Shit!'

He turned back to face the roadhouse and noticed that all the interior lights were doused. Another vehicle drove off somewhere behind the building, and then only the buzz of the floodlights competed with the noise of the myriad of insects encircling them.

This was clearly not good.

PIDGIN

Billy swayed silently on the steep shoulder of the highway.

What now?

Sullenly he turned and walked back down the road and into the relative security of the flood-lights. On the side of the highway was a battered road sign peppered with bullet holes. It read:

Welcome to the Middle of Nowhere.
Population:
Sheep: 22,500
Flies: 2,000,000 (approx.)
Humans: 6

So where were the humans? Not to mention the sheep. As far as he could ascertain he was the only living thing in the immediate vicinity, except for the insects. He took a deep breath, turned his back on the roadhouse and, facing the blackness beyond, tilted his head toward the sky. His eyes slowly became accustomed to the dark.

It was a hot, moonless night. Still. Deathly still. A cool wisp of breeze blew on his face. It made the hair stand up on the back of his neck. The buzz of the lights and bugs in the background sounded like a distant piece of industrial machinery running at high speed. He tuned it out and let the hushed darkness neutralise the noise. Silence closed in around him.

The stars. Billy had never seen anything like them. He had spent his entire life in the city and rarely ventured out into the country. Except for the fireworks on New Year's Eve, he had never seen so many points of light in the sky. He was astounded. There were millions of them. A thick band stretched from one side of the heavens to the other. It was as if someone had taken a wet paintbrush and flicked white droplets in a wide sweep. He felt tiny, dwarfed under the celestial canopy, no bigger than the insects circling the floodlights behind him. He also felt incredibly alone. He was used to the clamour and noise of the city. There was always someone around. You were never completely isolated. Even when it was quiet at night you could still hear the hum of distant traffic. This much silence was abnormal. It was almost tangible. He felt it pressing down on him. All he could hear now was the self-inflicted banging in his head, and his blood rushing past his eardrums. It was very unsettling.

For a moment he stared with a mixture of awe and bewilderment at the view above him. Then he lowered his gaze and a shiver ran down his spine. Standing in the glow of the roadhouse lights and on the opposite side of the highway was a figure. Billy sucked in his breath and held it. The figure appeared human at first. An Aboriginal man of in- discernible age. Its face was almost completely ob- scured by a long white beard, and it was slightly hunched over what appeared to be a metre-long club. Both its hands and its chin rested on the knobbled end of the club. However, the figure was, as far as Billy could make out, perfectly scaled down to about half the size of an average adult. It wore a long, dark cloak, draped loosely over its shoulders and stretching down to just below its knees. The cloak glowed strangely iridescent, reflecting the dim light from the roadhouse and appearing to subtly change colour as it flowed gently in the soft breeze. It was constructed entirely of feathers.

Two other features stood out. First, its unshod feet weren't feet at all; they were the talons of some kind of bird. Fascinated and transfixed by them, Billy watched as one of them flexed and grasped at the loose stones at the edge of the highway. The talon buried itself a little in the soft sand. The other feature that caught his attention was its eyes. In the shadows it was as if they produced their own source of light. Their piercing, bluish-green intensity cut through him.

Billy spluttered. He had forgotten to breathe. He took a few short gasps of air and attempted to compose himself. His head was swimming; the pounding in his temples had all but subsided to a dull thud.

He heard his own voice enquire in his head, *Who are you?*

To his surprise an answer came. 'You can call me Pidgin.'

Billy was unsure if the voice had come from within his own head or from across the road. The sound of blood rushing in his head increased in volume. It completely enveloped him. His eyes locked onto those of Pidgin and he was drawn into them. Billy felt inexplicably pulled towards the strange bird-man and took one cautious step forward. He placed one foot on the edge of the asphalt. The road was warm beneath his feet. It still harboured the heat from a day of baking in the sun.

Pidgin raised one hand, motioning Billy to stop. He held his ground.

Suddenly the deafening sound of a klaxon and a blinding light came from Billy's left. An enormous road train roared between the two figures. The associated wind lifted Billy into the air and sent him flying backwards. He crashed down heavily in the dust. The vehicle rumbled off into the distance. Billy lay spread-eagled on his back in the dirt, his heart pounding furiously. He waited for his heartbeat to slow before propping himself up onto his elbows. He peered through the dissipating bulldust towards the other side of the road. There was nothing. Pidgin had vanished.

THE INTERCEPTOR

Billy climbed painfully to his feet. Rubbing his hip and checking left and right for any other vehicles, he strode uncertainly to the centre of the highway. A single, rust-coloured feather floated down and came to rest on one of the dividing lines on the road. Billy stooped down and carefully picked it up. He closely scrutinised it, but there was nothing unusual about it. It was a perfectly ordinary feather. He slipped it into the back pocket of his stonewash jeans.

He turned back to face the roadhouse and was shocked to see that, just like Pidgin, it had also disappeared. A surge of panic rose up within him. He swung around frantically and tried to get his bearings. In the bright starlight and with his eyes accustomed to the dark, he could clearly make out the curve of a road. He couldn't tell if it was the same stretch of road on which he had previously been standing or a new one. Apart from the highway there were a few lone trees and some low, bush scrub, and that was about it. Now more than ever he truly was in the middle of nowhere.

What the hell is going on?

He began to wonder if this was the real world. Perhaps at any moment he would wake from a dream. He pinched himself hard on his forearm. The pain was genuine and restarted the throbbing in his head.

'Nope, that feels pretty real,' he said aloud, trying to reassure himself; but in doing so he startled himself with his own voice.

In the distance he heard a vehicle approaching.

'Better not be another truck,' he muttered.

It sounded like something significantly smaller. He waited in the centre of the road and watched as the headlights approached. As the car neared he waved wildly, but it didn't seem to be slowing down. He yelled loudly, squinting at the piercing headlights. The driver saw him at the last minute and swerved. Billy remained anchored to the ground, petrified. The vehicle missed him by a couple of metres. One set of wheels left the hard tarmac and buried themselves in the soft shoulder, causing the vehicle to careen sideways. With tyres screeching in protest, it slid to a stop facing the opposite direction, amid a cloud of dust and the smoke of burning rubber. The engine died with a splutter.

Billy was shaking violently but relieved that he was no longer alone. He shielded his eyes from the headlights and, after composing himself, walked slowly towards the vehicle.

He called out. 'Are you ok?'

A pair of male voices sounded from within the vehicle, one of them cursing loudly. 'What the fuck!'

The driver's door swung open with a loud squeal and someone wrenched themselves out of the car.

'You idiot, you could get y'self killed standing in the middle of the road like that!'

'Sorry, sorry, I'm a bit lost,' replied Billy timidly.

'That has to be the understatement of the century,' came the irritated reply. 'You scared the shit out o' me. What y' doing out here?'

Billy pondered the question for a moment.

'To be honest, I have no idea.'

'What'd he say?' a gruff voice inquired from within the vehicle.

'Think he's on drugs or someth'n.' Turning to Billy: 'So you just dropped out of the sky then?'

Billy considered telling the facts that he knew, but decided it would be wiser to keep them to himself. At the moment, extracting himself from his present predicament was his first priority, and further alienating his rescuers wouldn't help his cause.

'Just got dumped here and don't wanna go into it right now.'

'Girl trouble,' the driver remarked wryly to his accomplice, who responded with a snort. Both men then broke into a cackle.

Billy sensed that, apart from the initial shock, both men were relatively blasé about their close shave. He saw his opportunity. 'Can you give me a lift?'

The laughing abruptly stopped and the two men quietly discussed the situation. Billy stood for a moment, feeling very exposed in the bright light. He tried unsuccessfully to make out what they were saying. Eventually the discussion ended and the driver spoke up. 'Ok, mate, we can tell you're in a fix. We're on our way home and you can come with us. We'll find you somewhere to crash and sort the rest out in the morning.'

'Thanks a lot,' said Billy gratefully.

Up to this point he hadn't even laid eyes upon his rescuers. They were hidden behind a wall of light. He walked over to the driver's door and was slightly surprised to see a tall, thin Aboriginal man. His skin was the deepest tone of black.

'My name's Billy.'

'I'm Rob and this is Tex.' Rob motioned towards the shadow in the front seat.

The shadow's head was engulfed in an enormous Akubra stockman's hat and he barely acknowledged Billy's presence. Exasperated, he responded wearily, 'C'mon, I'm buggered. Let's get moving!'

'You'll have to put some elbow grease into the back door. It sticks a bit,' said Rob.

On his third attempt Billy managed to tug the door open. He slid into the seat, and it required the same amount of effort to close the door behind him. The car, a 1970s Ford Falcon, had seen better days. Billy hadn't had the opportunity to scrutinise its exterior, but surmised that the main material holding it together was rust. The rips in the vinyl of the backseat were almost deep enough to swallow him. Surprisingly, the front bench seat appeared to be in pristine condition.

'You might have to make a bit of room on the floor.'

Rob wasn't kidding. The entire floor well was filled to the brim with cans, bottles and other assorted rubbish. Billy tried his best to ignore it. 'My dad had one of these.'

'Is that right? It's my pride and joy, mate. Spend every spare moment I've got doing her up.' Rob puffed himself up like a penguin. 'Call her "The Interceptor"; you know, like Mel Gibson's car in *Mad Max*? Cousin of mine worked on the film over in Broken Hill a few years ago. He scored a few parts from one of the ones they wrecked.'

'So nobody uses the backseat?' Billy inquired, trying to find a stable space to rest his feet on top of the pile of rubbish.

'No, not yet, but I'm working on that too. Her name is Mabel.'

Tex chuckled. 'Mabel wouldn't be seen dead in this heap of shit, mate, not even in the front seat!'

'Ok, ok,' said Rob defensively. 'Let's get the old girl moving.'

He turned the ignition and the car roared into life, as did the cassette player. Slim Dusty blared out of the speakers, 'And the biggest disappointment in the world was me ...'

One of the speakers on the back shelf of the car was only a few centimetres from Billy's left ear. He instinctively pulled his head to one side and clapped his hands around his ears.

'Hey! Can you turn it down a bit!'

'Sorry,' Rob murmured sheepishly, and fiddled with the volume knob on the stereo. The speakers crackled loudly, followed by a reduction in the volume of the music. Slim launched into another verse. He reminisced about his travels. He sang about going without food and other hardships, and described how, once he eventually returned home, he had become a different man.

Rob swung the car around with some difficulty. He struggled with the big steering wheel and the lack of power steering. Once he was back on the road, he accelerated down the highway. They sat in silence for a while, listening to the music. Billy was not a fan of country music. He wasn't a country boy and felt quite alien sitting in a car with two characters that clearly were. He had met very few indigenous Australians in his time. This was probably the longest conversation he'd had with one of them. He was aware of the political arguments over land rights and the stolen generations, but it had never interested him. The men were as foreign to Billy as any of the overseas backpackers he met in his local bar. Even their use of the English language was a bit hard to follow. At the moment he was totally dependent on them. He had no idea where he was or where he was going, but he still appreciated their generosity. In the city this probably wouldn't have happened. There, it was every man for himself; or, at least, that had been his experience. Yet he felt a sort of kinship with his unknown saviours. He trusted them. They seemed honest and had taken everything in their stride, which was not at all like him. He was mistrustful of strangers and only spent time with his closest friends. He wasn't prone to taking risks and, under normal circumstances, he would probably have ignored these people if they had asked for help on the street. Even so, he could relate in part to Slim's words. He was clearly a long way from home and distance was certainly on his mind.

Rob slowed the car and turned onto a dirt side road. The previously smooth hum of tires on a sealed road turned into an undulating rumble. Rob called back, 'We're about a half-hour drive from here.'

'Cool!'

'Where you from?' Tex spoke up out of the gloom.

'Adelaide. Where are we going?'

'Uranda, little place west of Alice Springs.'

Alice Springs! Billy was flabbergasted. His mates had really pulled off a coup this time. He guessed they had expected him to wake up a lot earlier than he had. Still, at least now he had an inkling as to where he was. All was not completely lost, although he doubted there would be a bus stop where they were heading. Maybe in the morning he could find some way to get to Alice Springs and head home. With all that had happened to him, his head was swimming. Thoughts of his wife to be and the wedding flashed across his mind. It was all too much to consider and he pushed the thoughts away. He let his head rest back on the seat and stared out the window and up at the stars. The rocking of the car and occasional vibrations from the corrugations in the road sent Billy into a restless slumber.

A short time later Rob woke him with the announcement that they had arrived at their destination. Billy peered out the window. They were in a small town consisting of an assortment of prefabricated houses. There didn't seem to be a regular street plan. Just a few buildings scattered around and, as he had assumed, no sign of a bus stop. They pulled up at a small, single-roomed cabin constructed of white corrugated iron sheeting.

Rob stuck his arm through his window and indicated the small dwelling.

'You can sleep here tonight. It's open and the light switch is just inside the door. I'll come 'n' get y' in the morning and show you 'round.'

Billy, not yet fully awake, groggily murmured his thanks before extracting himself from the car. He resorted to kicking the uncooperative car door with both feet to open it, and it took all his strength to slam it shut again. He waved a half-hearted goodbye as the car pulled slowly away, before plodding up the few steps to the cabin and opening the door. He felt along the doorjamb and found a light switch. He turned it on, blinking at the sudden glare of fluorescent light.

The room was sparse but clean. In one corner was a small kitchenette, in the opposite a double bed. There was also a small table with two wooden chairs and a slightly overused, two-seater couch. He was exhausted and had lost all sense of time. Although it could only have been a couple of hours at most since he had stumbled off the bus, it felt like weeks. He glanced around the room again. Hanging on one wall was an Albert Namatjira print depicting a lone ghost gum with rolling hills in the background. The painting seemed to spring off the cream-coloured wall, its vivid pastel colours lighting up the rest of the otherwise barren room. Looking at it he felt better. It exuded its own warmth.

Billy let himself drop onto the bed. He tugged off his shoes and socks and threw them in one corner. He peeled off his jeans and flung them over one of the chairs at the table. He then lay on the bed and stared at the ceiling. A large huntsman spider was trying to make itself invisible in the crevice between the wall and the ceiling.

Realising that he had forgotten the light, Billy groaned and rolled out of bed. He took one step towards the door, reached out and flipped off the light switch. He sat back down on the bed and slowly leaned back. It was a relief to finally be able to stretch his body out full length. He settled himself and stared once again at the ceiling. Starlight was streaming softly through one small window. After a moment Billy closed his eyes, and within seconds he was asleep.

....

On the other side of the room Pidgin sat cross-legged on the small table, staring inquisitively at the motionless figure on the bed. He let his chin sink down onto his chest. His beard and coat became one. In the dim light it appeared as if there was a mound of feathers piled up on the kitchen table.

....

1969

I can feel him moving in my belly. I'm pretty sure it's a him. My mother could have told me for certain. He is strong. I can sense it by the way he kicks. He has spirit and will be a survivor.

Although he's not due for a couple of months they have put me in hospital. There is talk of complications but the doctors won't elaborate. I wish they would tell me what's going on. They have done a lot of tests and are continually taking blood and urine samples. Quite often I'm feverish and on a number of occasions I have had blackouts. There's more going on in my body than just a baby growing. Of this I'm sure. Something is taking hold of me and will not let go. Before the pregnancy I had begun training to be a nurse so I am familiar with hospitals. It irritates me that they won't tell me what's afflicting me. I can understand that they don't want to alarm me but I have already had to contend with so much in my life. This is something I can deal with. I will take it in my stride, as I have done with everything else. I am not so much afraid for myself as I am for him. I want him to live. I have a really strong feeling that he is destined for greatness, and that it is my responsibility to bring him safely into this world.

When the fever takes hold of me I start having the most vivid dreams. I keep seeing myself as a child. It was when we were still living the traditional way, out in the desert. My parents are there, and my brother. There are just snippets, though, and all very foggy. At the start of the dreams we are all together, and then towards the end a darkness descends and I find myself standing alone. Something happens out there and it is terrible. I just don't know what it is. My own memory of that time is very vague.

It's all very upsetting. It hurts so much to think about my family. I wish they were all here now but they were taken from me. This all happened long ago. I guess at the time I was only about six years old. I honestly don't know exactly when I was born, or where for that matter. I can remember being told that my parents were sick and that I wasn't allowed to be near them. I thought that just meant not seeing them until they got better, but once they took me away I never saw them again. That was before they taught me English, so maybe I didn't understand everything properly. My brother was also taken away and I have no idea what became of him. After the separation I recall crying myself to sleep at night for a long time afterwards. I felt so alone.

Most distressing of all is not being able to visualise my family's faces. The memories I have of those times are only loose pictures in my mind, like photos in an album. In the dreams I am seeing them all over again. Somehow it's the dreams that are giving those loose pictures more clarity. I can remember roaming the desert. I recall that it was a hard life but somehow we always pulled through. Although I can't see his face I do see my father laughing. He had such a broad grin. It makes me smile just thinking about the happiness that poured from him. He never seemed to worry. At least, that is my impression. He knew so much about the land and what it had to offer. I recall him showing my brother how to find water and teaching him how to make spears and other tools. He was very proud of his spear-throwing ability and would show off in front of my mother. I know she secretly admired his talents but would never let on. She would often speak secretly to me of his courage but never to his face. There was so much knowledge there. It is a shame it's all been lost. I'm sure if he'd had the chance he would have taught my brother more of the ways and we could have carried on as we were.

I also have memories of hunting for food with my mother. We would dig for ants and bush vege-tables. I cannot recall us ever going hungry, even when my father returned from hunting without a catch. My mother would tell me stories and sing songs about the old ways. I wish I could remember her stories but my memory fails me. It was so long ago and I was so very young. I wish she was here now to help and guide me with bringing my child into this world. I'm sure she would know what to do.

After we were separated from one another they put me in a home. There were a lot of children there just like me. We came from all over the place. It was some consolation that we'd all been through the same thing, being separated from our parents and all. We could at least provide each other a bit of comfort. Most of the time I just kept to myself and tried not to attract attention. The sisters that ran the home were very strict and dealt out harsh pun-ishment if you stepped out of line. I did make some friends there, though, and we still try to stay in contact. At the home they taught us a lot of things, like how to wash and clean, how to keep house. It was as if they were preening us to be dutiful housewives, or perhaps something even more menial. I do have to thank them for teaching me to read and write, though. Without those skills who knows where I would have ended up. They also drilled the Word of God into us. I'm certain my first English words were those from a hymn. When I was young I believed what they told me. I had no point of reference. Now I am starting to see things differently. The old memories are flooding back through my dreams. Perhaps it also has a lot to do with this new responsibility, bringing my own child into the world. It is now no longer only about me but also about him.

This country has changed so much since my childhood. I do know that I came from somewhere in the north of South Australia but very little else. I don't know the name of our tribe, or even if they still exist. I have been brought up to forget those things. However, I can't completely forget; it's a part of me. My dreams reinforce this. Hopefully one day things will be different and I will be able to go back and find out about my heritage. At the very least I will try to instil this in my son, although I'm sure it will be difficult.

A few months ago I married a white man. He decided it was the right thing for us to do after discovering I was pregnant. He is a good man. He is kind and dotes on me, but he doesn't understand what I've been through. This is not surprising. We come from very different worlds. Before I met him I thought I would go it alone. I was going to study hard and find a good job. Until I became pregnant I was a trainee nurse at this very hospital. The training was difficult but I was pleasantly surprised to find that I have a great capacity to learn. It also helped that a couple of the girls from the home were studying with me. One of them is even attending to me now. So there are some positives, I guess. I don't know that I completely trust the doctors, though. Especially because they don't seem to want to tell me about my condition. Through my working experience here I know that they do their best for people, so I find it strange that they are not communicating. Maybe they just don't know. At least I can rely on my friend. She is my eyes and ears, trying to find out what is going on.

Now that I'm having a child I'm afraid that I will need to put my aspirations of becoming a nurse aside, at least for the moment. My main priority is the safety of my baby. I don't want to lose him as my mother lost me. It's fortunate that I am married as that will keep the inspectors away. I need to ensure that our relationship survives, as it will affect what happens to my child. I have heard that they still come and take children away for no good reason. It's best if I continue to live as I have been and keep my secrets to myself. If I keep my head down and use the friends I have, my child will be safe.

He is kicking again. Oh what power he has. I will whisper to him. It usually calms him to hear my voice. I'm certain that it won't be long before I see his face. And his will be a face I surely will never forget.

TWO

....

THE COMMUNITY

THE DAY AFTER

Billy opened his eyes. Everything was white. He slowly reached out his hand and felt a cool, hard wall centimetres from his face. He was alive.

'Thank God!' He exhaled.

He sensed something behind him and, pushing himself away from the wall with both hands, rolled over and swung his legs out of bed. His bare feet slapped the floor, jarring his ankles and causing him to wince. The bed was much lower than he had expected. He looked around the room. It was just as he vaguely remembered it from the night before. Something was lying on the table. With both hands on his knees he leant forward, letting his own weight pivot him into a standing position. He walked to the table and scooped up a feather. Curious, he reached down for his discarded jeans.

Searching through its pockets he found what he was looking for. Pulling out the feather he had picked up the previous night, he laid them side by side on the table. He inspected them as if they were two pieces of criminal evidence. They were the same. A shiver ran down his spine.

The short meeting with Pidgin had truly unsettled him. He wasn't completely sure what he had seen. After all, he hadn't been entirely sober and the effects of an enormous hangover had dulled his senses. At any rate, it was clear that Pidgin had meant him no harm. He had even gone a step further and prevented him from becoming roadkill. However, Billy surmised, he probably wouldn't have found himself on the highway in the first place if Pidgin hadn't been there to attract his attention.

Even though his senses had been diminished he was relatively sure that Pidgin was real, or real enough. He had physical evidence to attest to this. What concerned him now was the feeling that he had been followed. He had found another feather. He picked them up and inspected them once more. They were exactly the same. He was no bird expert, though, and the second feather could have been there all along. He had gone straight to bed the night before and not really taken a good look at the room. The best thing would be just to wait and see if Pidgin appeared again. Billy wasn't certain that this would happen, but he was convinced that the sudden strange apparition had a purpose. If Pidgin presented himself again he could try to confront him or detain him long enough to get more information.

Billy pushed the thoughts from his mind and attempted to focus on the here and now.

He was in a small, outback community. There was a bastion of civilisation, Alice Springs, somewhere in the vicinity. There were people he could call on for assistance. At least, he hoped this was the case. He still had to step outside. There was the minor chance that he would find himself in another place altogether. He decided to keep positive and trust that no more radical changes had occurred while he was asleep. He was starving hungry. He desperately needed to have a piss.

'Shit, where's the loo?'

He frantically looked around the room. His bladder was ready to burst. There were only two doors, the one he had come in through and one to the side of the small kitchen. He made a beeline for the door in the kitchen. He wrenched it open and was gratified to see a small bathroom with a toilet in one corner. After momentarily struggling with his underwear, he relieved himself, letting out a long sigh in the process. He pulled up his pants and turned to a small basin next to the toilet. He turned the tap, half expecting there to be no water. After some spluttering, water gushed into the basin. It looked clean and pure, unlike the water from the roadhouse. He splashed some on his face and ran his fingers through his hair. He then cupped his hands under the flow and drank deeply. He turned off the tap, straightened up and decided to go in search of sustenance.

Back in the kitchen he opened cupboards. They were particularly barren except for the very basics: salt, pepper and sugar cubes. He popped a sugar cube in his mouth and sucked thoughtfully on it. It made his teeth ache but he was rewarded with a small surge of energy. He turned to examine the refrigerator. Disappointingly it was completely empty, and looking behind it he noted it wasn't even plugged in. He wasn't going to get far on basic condiments. He would just have to take the plunge and confront the great unknown beyond the cabin door. He walked across the room, pulled on his jeans, socks and shoes. Sticking his nose under an armpit he inhaled deeply. He was on the positive side of what was permissible in personal hygiene, but only barely. With a heightened sense of pur-pose he walked to the door and flung it open.

Harsh sunlight temporarily blinded him, coupled with a fierce blast of superheated desert air. He reached desperately for the door and pulled it shut.

'Gonna need more sugar!'

Billy grabbed a handful of cubes and stuffed them in his pocket before flicking one deftly into his mouth. Then, without hesitation, he opened the front door and jumped outside.

THE GUITARIST

Billy could hear music. Shading his eyes with one hand, he took a quick look around. His eyes slowly adjusted to the glare and he took in his surroundings. In the broad light of day things didn't look substantially different from the night before. Several single-storey buildings were scattered around him. Most were constructed of white, corrugated iron and were particularly modest. There were none of the usual things associated with the suburban houses he was used to. There were no gardens, no swathes of verdant lawn, no flower beds; nothing even to tell them apart. They were all the same, simple, little white boxes, with a small verandah tacked on the front. They could have been uninhabited. In fact, if it hadn't been for the music, he would have assumed the whole town was deserted. There were no street signs, or even streets, for that matter. Just a hotchpotch of dwellings spread sparsely among a few particularly sad and dried out trees.

Billy focussed on the sound. It wasn't difficult to work out where it was coming from as it was the only discernible noise in his immediate vicinity. Through the trees he could make out a relatively large building, also constructed of corrugated iron. It differed from the other dwellings in that it was unpainted and had the appearance of a garden shed, only a good deal bigger. He honed his hearing and was reasonably sure the sound was emanating from within. He decided to investigate. After all, it didn't seem that Rob would miraculously appear out of nowhere and meet him as arranged. He couldn't easily get lost here, and if all else failed he could return to the cabin. He made a mental note of its number. A hand-carved representation of the number three hung next to the cabin door. It was coated in faded brown paint, which seemed to be peeling off before his eyes. The heat was oppressive and he was melting on the spot. He felt some affinity with the paint. Sweat formed on his brow, even though he was standing perfectly still and had barely exerted himself. He hoped the giant garden shed would provide some form of refuge.

Billy set out with some haste, leaving a cloud of fine, red dust in his wake. He crossed an open area before ducking between some trees and heading towards the shed, which he now saw had two large doors. One of them had been carelessly flung open. It swayed a little on its rusted hinges in the warm breeze, emitting a small peep, not unlike a native bird. He stepped inside and immediately felt a marked drop in temperature.

The shed, which could better be described as a hall, was quite large. The only illumination was provided by sunlight streaming in behind him through the open door. The relatively cavernous space was set up as a mini theatre, with about a hundred well-worn folding chairs forming an audience area. A narrow, crooked aisle snaked its way between the chairs, dividing them down the middle. His eyes followed his own long shadow, cast down it by the light streaming in behind him. At the far end of the shed was a stage. The stage was raised about a metre and a half above the audience area and, apart from one feature, was empty. On the stage, on a wobbly chair, which appeared as if it would collapse at any moment, sat a figure, rocking backwards and forwards and hunched over an electric guitar. His face was obscured by a wide-brimmed Akubra stockman's hat and he was completely immersed in playing his guitar, oblivious to his surroundings. Next to him was a small amplifier which emitted an incredible amount of noise. The noise filled the hall, almost to the point of bursting. It seemed as if the walls themselves were arching outwards and threatening to buckle under the strain. Billy considered himself a bit of a music aficionado and it sounded to him for all the world like Stevie Ray Vaughan going hell for leather. The music had its roots in the country genre but with a definite blues/rock influence. He was impressed. He stood in the aisle for a moment and, half closing his eyes, let the music flow over him. He rocked gently, pivoting on his ankles.

The music stopped. Billy opened his eyes. The guitarist was staring right at him, his eyes just visible beneath the brim of his hat. A voice called out from within the shadows in a corner to his right and a few rows from the front of the stage.

'Did you have a good kip?'

Billy took a few tentative steps towards the stage and recognised Rob on one of the chairs, sitting with two other young Aboriginal men.

'Yeah, good thanks.'

'Come in and enjoy the concert.'

Billy looked up at the guitarist and realised this must be Rob's passenger, Tex, from the night before. The amplifier was buzzing loudly. Tex reached over and adjusted some of the knobs, pulled his hat down over his eyes, and launched into another distorted blues riff.

Billy walked over to Rob who yelled out, trying to make himself heard over the cacophony. 'Take a seat, mate!'

Billy accepted his invitation and sat beside him. He slid up close to him to hear what he was saying.

'So, how you feeling?'

'Oh, I'm ok. Well, I'm pretty hungry actually.'

'Well I guess we'd better do someth'n about that. This is Daniel and Matthew.' He indicated the two young men sitting next to him. Billy nodded to them and they reciprocated.

'Daniel's gonna open up the shop soon; then you can get some tucker.'

'Great!'

It occurred to him that he wasn't even sure if he had any money. He sensed the bulge of his wallet in his back pocket. It prodded uncomfortably into his right buttock and he was somewhat reassured. He hoped there was still something of value in it apart from the wad of worthless receipts he invariably accumulated.

They all turned to face the stage.

'Is that Tex up there?'

'Yep. He's not bad, eh?'

'Yeah, he's pretty damn good. I play a bit of guitar myself.'

'Really? Maybe you two should have a jam.'

Before Billy had time to consider the offer, Rob had stood up and, edging past him, marched purposely towards the stage.

'C'mon.' He waved for Billy to follow and pointed beneath the stage. 'We've got heaps of equipment under here.'

Rob got down on his knees and stuck his head under the stage. Billy joined him in inspecting the underside of the stage. Rob was correct. There was a lot of musical equipment there, a few amplifiers and a couple of guitar cases. There was also what seemed like a complete drum kit. Everything was dusty and didn't look as though it had been used for some time. However, everything, including the chairs, was coated in the same fine dust. Billy concluded it was a result of the environmental conditions rather than a lack of interest in the equipment. Rob moved one of the amplifiers to one side to give better access to a guitar case before moving back. Affixed to the back of the amplifier was a number of what seemed like small, white cotton balls.

'Better watch out for them.' Rob pointed at the balls. 'They're red-back spider eggs. The mum is probably hanging round here somewhere. They're pretty defensive, you know.'

Billy had been stung numerous times as a child by bees and had developed an aversion to anything from the arthropod community. He shrank back from the amplifier and out from under the stage.

'I'm not that good a guitarist. Just a beginner really.' Sensing that he might be insulting Rob's generous offer he added, 'To be perfectly honest, I've really got to get something in my stomach first.'

As if on cue, his stomach let out a long, low growl. Self consciously, Billy clasped his hands to it in a vain effort to silence it.

'Sorry, mate, had forgotten you needed some tucker. We can do this later. Let's see if we can get you someth'n.'

They stood and dusted off the knees of their jeans. Rob walked over to Daniel and said something to him, all the while motioning towards Billy. He beckoned Billy over. 'Daniel will get you sorted. I'll catch up with you later. I should really be doing some odd jobs at the moment.'

Billy thanked him and, following Daniel's lead, walked across to the doorway of the shed. He stopped for a moment. Looking back he took the scene in one last time. Up on stage Tex was totally immersed in a world of his own. He was now arching his back with his eyes half closed. His fingers glided effortlessly over the fretboard. He was also shaking his head with such ferocity that Billy was amazed that the Akubra remained fixed to his skull. Watching Tex in full flight brought a smile to Billy's face. He also felt a sharp pang of jealousy. What a life this was, so relaxed and carefree, unlike anything he was used to.

With regret Billy wrenched himself away from the scene. He followed Daniel outside, steeling himself once more against the renewed onslaught of heat and bright light.

THE GENERAL STORE

The store was dank and cool. The floor a simple plateau of polished concrete. It was like being in a freezer compared to the environment outside.

Daniel had taken his time opening up the store. He walked around flipping on switches before going behind the counter and turning on the till. Fluorescent lights flickered to life and made their presence known. Their starkness shone down from above but, with no white walls to reflect them, they barely penetrated into the far recesses of the store. Billy was used to brightly lit supermarkets with placards everywhere, enticing the clientele to spend more than they wanted. This was much simpler: three wide aisles, long and dimly lit. Well-worn price tags were stuck at irregular intervals on the shelves. The lettering on many of them had severely faded and was barely legible.

Billy was famished but didn't know what to eat. He checked along the aisles. The shelves were filled, but only sparsely. Any shopping done here was for incidental items, things that had been forgotten on a trip to a better stocked supermarket. There were all the basics but nothing whet his appetite. Breakfast cereals weren't at all tempting: they involved milk and his stomach was still recovering from the effects of his late night out. The abundance of canned food also wasn't appealing. That would mean having to use a pot to warm one of them up. He also didn't recall seeing a can opener during his search for food at the cabin and decided it wouldn't be worth the struggle. At home he had been confronted with the same situation a number of times. He also didn't possess a can opener and had often resorted to using other kitchen utensils. Invariably a large percentage of the contents of the dreaded can never reached their intended destination. He could picture a kitchen floor doused in baked beans and decided he didn't want to go there.

The prudent thing was to first take stock of his financial situation. This would dictate what he could or could not purchase. Towards the middle of the store he found a slightly rusted, waist-high ice-cream freezer with a sliding glass lid. It was stocked with a limited variety of products. He rummaged through his pockets, turning them out one by one and laying the contents on the lid. In his front pocket he found some loose change—he estimated about three dollars—and his house keys. In one back pocket he found the two feathers. His other back pocket was bulging. He took a deep breath and mentally crossed his fingers before pulling everything out. He spread it all out on the freezer lid.

There was his misshapen wallet, a battered affair which had seen better days, and an envelope. As he had suspected, his wallet contained mostly worthless paper receipts, most of which he had no idea what purchase they were connected to. He screwed them up in a tight ball and made a mental note to discard them. He didn't quite understand why receipts had been invented. You really didn't need to keep track of every soft drink and stick of chewing gum you bought.

The envelope was the one paper container which may be of some use. It was crinkled and half folded, having taken on the shape and curvature of his posterior. It was sealed and he carefully peeled it open. Inside was a crisp—or, at least, it had been before living in his pocket—hundred-dollar note. He whooped and punched the air before looking around self-consciously. From the front of the store Daniel gave Billy a wide grin. Billy's face flushed.

He pulled the money out of the envelope, together with a piece of paper. On it was scrawled, in sloping handwriting: 'Merry Wedding Day! Have a nice life and don't forget about us, Your Mates!!'

His wedding day. By his own calculations that should have been today. He felt a pang of guilt mixed with fear. His fiancée was going to skin him alive if he ever made it back to her. He pushed the thought quickly aside. Facing her wrath would certainly come, but right now he had other concerns. Billy surmised that his friends had planned this ahead of time. At least, that was the impression the money and note gave him. Thankfully they had presented him with a way to get home. Although they probably wouldn't have expected him to have travelled so far. He started to feel a bit better about his predicament. He was fairly certain he could make the money stretch until he found his way home. Nevertheless, he was cautious about how much he should outlay for the present.

He slid the money and note carefully into the recesses of his wallet for safekeeping. He picked up the feathers and studied them once more. They seemed to have changed colour, taking on a bright, bronze hue. Disconcerted, Billy shook his head. He was certain they had been light grey and quite plain; definitely not as spectacular as they were now. He put it down to the different light in the store. Or it might have something to do with the fact that he had just woken up when he had previously examined them. At that stage he had yet to gain complete control of his faculties. This reminded him to concentrate seriously on the task he had set himself. He returned them to his pocket for later analysis and scooped up the loose change before recommencing his search for breakfast.

He walked to the back of the store. The rear wall was completely filled with a long line of glass doors. Behind the frosted glass he could make out sections with juices, soft drinks, water, dairy products and frozen food. This was the best-stocked area of the entire store. Strangely, there was no beer. Of all the places where you could kill for one, this would be it. He walked along the wall and came upon the meat section. Bending down a little he could make out some long shapes on the bottom shelf. He opened the door to get a better look but was still unable to work out what they were. They looked like huge, furry sausages and were at least a metre long. Billy began to have doubts about the store's standard of hygiene. If they were sausages then their present state went far beyond any laboratory experiment with bacteria. He could personally attest to this based on his own experimentation with neglected food in his cupboards at home.

'Kangaroo tails.'

Billy stood up in surprise. On the other side of the open glass door was a small, well-rounded Aboriginal woman. Her face was beaming and she exuded such warmth and joviality that he couldn't help but smile back.

'They're kangaroo tails.'

'Oh?'

'Good tucker. You burn off the fur and bury 'em in the ground with some hot coals. Depending on where you're from you eat 'em rare or well done. Either way it takes a few hours.'

'I-I'm Billy,' he stuttered. The last thing he had expected was someone to advise him on the finer points of bush culinary procedure.

'I know. Hear Rob's been taking care of you.'

'That's right.'

'Bit lost are we?'

'You could say that.'

Behind the well-informed little woman a much younger woman stepped from one of the aisles. She was tall and slender and quite beautiful. He took particular note of her hands: her fingers were long and well manicured. She looked out of place in her surroundings. He could picture her back in the city where she could easily have passed for a model.

'Got what you wanted, Auntie?'

'Yep. Just a minute. Need some eggs.'

She stepped around the door and, reaching past Billy, pulled out a carton of eggs.

'Be seeing you 'round, I guess?'

'Ahem, dunno. I'm kind of looking for a way home.'

'Well, I hope you find it.'

Billy nodded at her and both women returned to the front of the shop. Billy, in a trance, held the freezer door open and watched them leave. He began to feel the chill of the freezer, and, shivering, slammed the door shut and rubbed his arms to warm them up, before finishing his promenade of the freezers. At one end he found the chocolate section. Not able to make a decision, he reached in and grabbed the first thing at eye level: a Mars Bar. He thought for a minute before grabbing a second one. 'Gonna have to do for now.'

He walked to the front of the store and laid the chocolate bars on the counter. 'Who were they?' He gestured with his head towards the two women who had just left.

'Oh, that was Auntie Doris. She's like an elder around here.'

'An elder?'

'Well, were still pretty big on traditions around here. It's like we're all one big family and she's kind of a mother to all of us. She knows a lot about the old ways and teaches us stuff.'

'And the girl?'

'That'd be Mabel.'

Now Billy could understand Rob's infatuation. Mabel was a striking woman.

'Mabel? Rob's girl then?'

'Na. He'd like to think so, but they're just mates. They couldn't have anything to do with each other anyway; they're both from the same skin.'

'Skin?'

'Yeah, that's also a tradition. You're not allowed to marry anyone from your own family is basically what it's all about.'

'But you said you were all family?'

'Well, we're all kinda from the same tribe. The tribe is made up of a few families and you can marry into another family, but not your own.'

'Interesting. Makes sense, I guess.'

'You gonna pay for that?'

'Oh, sorry, yeah.'

Billy dug deep into his pocket and pulled out the loose change. He dropped it on the counter with a clatter. Daniel slapped his hand down on the coins to stop them rolling off the counter and proceeded to count out what he needed. He then slid the remaining coins back across the counter.

'Thanks.'

'No worries.'

Billy unwrapped the chocolate bar with relish. He eyed it for a moment and took a large bite before strolling outside.

DOUG AND THE STORM

The glare that hit Billy as he passed through the double doors was like a slap in the face. A stark difference from the store's dim interior. Night had become day in an instant. It seemed as if the sun was situated on the other side of the street and not somewhere millions of kilometres away in the heavens. The heat was more intense than before. He stepped out onto the wide verandah which shaded the facade of the shop and nearly tripped over a robust, middle-aged Aboriginal man sitting on the steps leading down to street level. The man was in mid sentence. He was extremely animated and gesticulated broadly as he spoke. Billy attempted to say sorry but with his mouth still full only managed a spray of Mars Bar. The man seemed unperturbed, and after a slight pause continued telling his story with even more gusto. Billy took a half step backwards and bumped into Daniel coming out of the store. He grunted an apology through closed lips, not wanting to lose any more of his breakfast.

As his eyes slowly grew accustomed to the piercing, midday sun he surveyed the street from under his eyebrows. He was taken aback. The deserted town had miraculously transformed into a thriving metropolis. There were people everywhere. A number of small children and young adults sat in a tight semi-circle on the ground in front of the man and were listening intently to his story. The rest of the main street was a hive of activity. At a glance Billy estimated that there were over a hundred people gathered on the street. There was a lot of noise. Small pockets of people were gathered in groups, deep in loud conversation. There were peals of laughter everywhere. It had the air of a large family reunion.

'What's going on?' he inquired of Daniel.

'It's Welfare Day. Everyone's here to pick up their cheques.'

'Where did they all come from?'

'Oh, pretty much from all over the place.'

'Don't any of them have jobs?'

Daniel looked at him incredulously, clearly insulted.

'It's pretty hard going out here, mate. It's not like we want it this way. We'd really like to get off of government handouts but it's difficult. Maybe you should have a chat to Doug here.' He waved his hand, indicating the man Billy had nearly tripped over. 'He can explain it better than me.'

Billy looked down at Doug and decided it wasn't a good moment to interrupt him. He was in full flight and had a captive audience. Daniel, on the other hand, clearly didn't feel restricted by etiquette. Unperturbed he stepped forward and gave Doug a gentle nudge.

'Fella here, wants to know why we're bludging off the dole.'

Billy protested. 'No, no, that's not what I meant.'

Doug seemed unruffled by the interruption and grinned widely up at him, 'Take a seat.'

Sheepishly Billy obliged and sat on the step next to him. Doug laid a hand on his shoulder. It was big and warm, and somehow felt very comforting, almost fatherly.

'I was just telling the kids about this. My father took over this land years ago. First they tried to grow grapes. You know, the eating kind. We worked for years on it. Had to cart water from miles away. It was pretty upsetting when it didn't work out. Problem was, the termites got to them. All we ended up with was firewood. Since then we've turned our hand to cattle and have a bit of a farm set up out there.'

He swept his arm in front of him. Behind the houses on the other side of the street Billy could only make out trees and low scrub. It all looked incredibly dry and lifeless, not the sort of land that would support anything of much substance. The idea of grape vines growing in such an environment perplexed him. He remembered how lush the Barossa Valley was, the wine-growing region north of Adelaide. It wasn't conceivable that anything could survive for very long out there. The whole idea struck him as ludicrous. Billy took another bite of his chocolate bar. He could feel the sugar starting to course through his body and began to feel somewhat revived.

'Right now we're busy sett'n up a bit of a studio so we can make pottery. We want to become self-sufficient but need a bit of help to get it all up and running. We really don't want to be reliant on government support. Everything you do with 'em comes at a price. We wanna run things ourselves.'

Doug spoke with an air of solid self-belief. He was fiercely passionate about this. Billy had the impression that Doug was a man capable of anything he put his mind to, that he could tackle and overcome any adversity. He hadn't intended to pass judgement, but still wasn't completely convinced that anyone could make something out of such a desolate place. It all seemed so barren and isolated.

Doug turned his attention back to his audience and continued to tell his story. Billy tuned out of the conversation and was preoccupied with the possibility that people could eke out an existence in such a place. He couldn't fathom how anything could survive in the desert, let alone flourish. He looked at the layer of red dust on his sneakers. They had been in pristine condition a day ago, white and shining. He had only bought them a few days before that. Now they seemed to have merged into their new surroundings. He wondered if he was capable of achieving the same transformation.

A sudden gust of wind rose and turned into something more intense. The dust in the main street was whipped up into mini tornadoes which began dancing up and down the road. The sudden, alarming drop in air pressure was palpable. The oppressive heat waned.

Billy stepped into the street and walked to the middle of the road. Turning back he could make out an undulating mountain range rising up behind the general store. Beyond the hills black storm clouds were forming. They were gigantic and seemed to be growing steadily in altitude and breadth before his eyes. He stood in awe. He had never experienced such a swift change in the weather. Looking at the looming clouds he felt incredibly small and exposed, like a scared boy on his first day at school.

The street around him was a sudden hive of activity. People ran around, some hurriedly getting into nearby vehicles. Gone was the calm, friendly atmosphere of a moment ago, to be replaced by a scene of mild panic. Clearly everyone was expecting a ferocious storm and getting out while there was still time.

In the middle of the street one figure stood absolutely still, his eyes focused on Billy. In an instant Billy felt isolated and detached from the bustle around him. He stood rooted to the spot with the chocolate bar slowly melting in his hand. It felt odd being so static with everyone else running around them. No one seemed aware of them. They stood motionless, staring at each other. He envisioned himself in an old cowboy movie, standing on a wind-swept main street and waiting for the opposition to draw his pistol. Only the figure wasn't carrying a pistol. He was leaning nonchalantly on a short club. The night before Billy had only seen Pidgin in the semi-darkness. It was a surprise to now see him in the broad light of day. He didn't seem out of place at all, just another person on the main street, except that he was standing stock still. He was dressed as Billy had remembered him, his cloak billowing with every wind gust. It was almost as if they had been transported from their first meeting and dumped into new surroundings. A large cloud of dust swirled down the street past Billy and continued on towards Pidgin. It obscured Billy's view of him and he squinted through the fine particles, trying to see him. Billy choked on a mouthful of dust and coughed loudly, trying to clear his throat. By the time he had recovered the dust had cleared and Pidgin had vanished.

Billy snapped back into motion. He looked around, trying to see if Pidgin was amongst the other people. Through the chaos and dust it was difficult to see anything clearly. Pidgin was nowhere to be seen. Billy felt a tap on his shoulder and wheeled around. It was Rob.

'You gonna eat that?'

'Huh?'

Rob indicated the chocolate bar. Its contents had melted and were oozing out of the wrapper and over Billy's hand. He looked down at it for a moment, peeled back the wrapper and wolfed down what was left of the contents. He licked the wrapper, scrunched it into a ball and stuffed it in his pocket. He wiped his hand down the leg of his jeans and looked up at Rob.

'Breakfast,' he said.

'Uh-huh. Hey mate, we're heading into town. You wanna come with us?'

'Town?'

'Alice Springs, mate.'

Billy was caught off guard. He was still trying to take in what he had just seen. He wrinkled his forehead and tried to process Rob's offer. With all the activity, he sensed that if he didn't take Rob up on it he would be left alone in the town. Everyone seemed to be clearing out. Up to this point he had let outside events guide his movements. He decided that the approach had worked well. It was probably best just to go with the flow and follow whatever opportunities arose. Anyway, there weren't many alternatives. It also dawned on him that he still needed to tackle the problem of his wedding.

'Ok, great. That would be really cool. Need to get to a phone and call my girlfriend.'

'I knew it,' Rob beamed with a satisfied grin. 'Girl trouble. Well c'mon then. The car's over here.'

Billy followed him down the street and around a corner. The Ford was parked under a tree which offered some welcome but scant shade. In the daylight the car stood out in stark contrast to its surroundings. Inexpertly painted bright, canary yellow it had rusted fringes. The sections that weren't in the shade glinted in the intense sunlight, and before he even laid a hand on it he knew the bodywork would be extremely hot. Billy recalled the previous night and braced himself for a struggle with the rear door. There was the added complication of trying not to burn himself on the door handle. To his surprise he was relatively successful. He expeditiously snatched at the handle and wrenched the door open in one fluid movement. He slid into the back seat and slammed the door behind him. He made a mental note to take the same decisive approach next time. He wasn't prepared to let something as insignificant as a car door slow him down.

Tex sat up front in the passenger's seat. Billy wondered if he ever sat anywhere else. He mused that the shape of his arse was probably permanently imprinted in the bench seat. Rob slid into the driver's seat. He turned the ignition and gunned the engine, gently eased the large vehicle out from under the tree, and turned onto the now-deserted main street. Heading past a few houses he drove to the outskirts of town. Billy attempted to wind down his window. The air was stifling in the vehicle. Air conditioning apparently wasn't one of the car's endearing features. The winder didn't move easily and the whole mechanism felt clogged with desert sand. He could feel it grinding as he tried to coax the handle. He tentatively put his full weight behind it and mercifully it yielded. The breeze that blew in through the window, although hot, was a welcome relief.

The main street swiftly expanded into a wide, dirt road lined with small trees. Billy turned to look out the rear window and watched as the town slipped from view behind the trees. An ever increasing cloud of dust rose behind them, eventually concealing everything in their wake. Billy's last glimpse of the town was of it shrinking beneath the imposing, blackening sky and being enveloped in a blanket of red dust.

EMU FIELD

....

1957

My family and I had been travelling for more than one cycle of seasons, since before the dingo pups were born. We had set out from Bonyboninnya and headed towards where the sun sets. At the time I did not agree with my fellow tribesmen regarding living off the invaders food and drink. I could see that they were giving up their traditional ways too easily and I didn't want to be a part of that. The decision to leave my totem home came when my tribesmen had speared and killed a bullock. I could understand the temptation to do this as the meat from a cow could nourish the entire tribe for a few days. Because the invaders had brought in their own animals our usual food sources were depleted, or had been forced away. Although it was an act of desperation I could not condone it. I also feared reprisals from the stockmen. In the past some of our men had been taken away to answer for what they had done. Many of them had never returned. I feared for the safety of myself and my family and was certain that we would find good hunting if we moved to other lands. So I decided to head further out into the desert and away from the influence of the invaders.

Upon arriving at Tepata I saw hunting fires towards the setting sun. Not knowing who these people were and not wanting to take the risk that they were hostile, I decided to follow the water lines towards the soak at Ooldea. I was hoping to find some of my relatives there. Ooldea was also the place where I had met and married my wife. In the past it had offered sanctuary. I hoped we could at least replenish our water and maybe get some food there before continuing our journey.

At some point we passed through a strange area. There were no signs of life, no ground animals and no birds. There was an odd silence which was unfamiliar to me. Before entering the area my wife had been able to find some honey ants and that had kept us going, along with the goanna I had speared a few days before. I continued to search for water. Unfortunately, the soak I had expected to find had been disguised by the shifting sands. As a boy my father had taught me all the names and positions of the rockholes and soaks. I also have them carved into my spears. For some reason the landscape I knew here as a young man had changed beyond recognition. It distressed me that my knowledge in this area was now of no use.

We then came to a place where the trees were no longer pointing towards the sky but were bent to the ground. They lay flattened, as if a giant wind had swept them over in its path. The earth under our feet was also odd. It was almost as if the sand itself had been ground to the fineness of ochre. It was black and slightly oily. There was also a peculiar smell, not unlike the odour of a dead kangaroo. It hung in the air. Even the stiff breeze that was blowing at the time could not diminish it. It was so strong that it bit into my nostrils when I inhaled. I found some rabbits and they were very easy to kill. They were crawling around aimlessly, unable to find their burrows. They seemed to have been struck blind. After some thought we decided against eating them. It was better that we go hungry than risk suffering from the same thing which ailed the rabbits. The sun began to set and we decided to camp for the night. We dared not move further in the darkness for fear of what else we would encounter.

During the night my familiar, Pidgin, appeared before me. He was silent but his very presence signalled that some form of danger was approaching. I wish now that I had heeded his warning and been more attentive.

The following morning we continued on through the trees and came upon a large clearing. At its centre was a raised mound in the form of a low, flat-topped hill. This hill was unfamiliar to me and I was sure it hadn't previously been there. I feared for the safety of my wife, daughter and son and so left them by the trees and ventured out into the open alone. I climbed the steep sides of the hill and stood on top. It was taller than the height of one man. To my surprise I found myself on the edge of a perfectly circular rockhole. It was as wide as twenty men laid out head to toe. It was full of water and very deep. This was extremely odd. The only water I had known of in this part of the desert was beneath the ground. The soaks were hard to find and often you would have to dig very deep. There had been substantial rain over the past season but usually the desert sands quickly absorbed it. I took a closer look at the edge of the lake. It was solid and shone in the sun. It was also very smooth and had the appearance of the invaders' drink containers. They called them bottles and I knew that the material they were made from was called glass. I took a long drink of the water but it didn't taste so good, so I decided not to let my wife and children drink it.

At that moment I heard a noise in the distance. Coming out of the trees in the opposite direction from which we had arrived was a small group of figures draped entirely in white. Even their heads were covered and they wore something on their faces. I was very much afraid and thought they were bad spirits. Nevertheless, I prepare to defend myself with my spear. Then one of them called out to me. He was talking to me in the invaders' language and from what I could understand it seemed he wanted me to go with them. With some hesitation I went to them, and on closer inspection I realised they were men and not of the spirit world at all. I had the feeling that they were as surprised to see me as I was to see them. I made them understand that I was not alone. They followed me and together we went to get my family.

They put us in one of their machines and transported us to their village. I had seen their machines before but had never been in one. We were all crammed together in the back of this apparatus. When it took off it felt as if I was being launch through the air and down a steep hill. I felt my stomach rise to my throat. I was petrified, as were my wife and children. They all began crying. It took all my courage to maintain my own composure and show that I was strong for them. The fear inside me was so great I felt I would die. I had never travelled at such a high speed. It was if we flew through the air like an eagle.

Before long we were all violently ill, my wife and son in particular. Thankfully, because of this, the men stopped the machine. They let us get out and gave us time to recover. I saw the fear in my daughter's eyes but also the desire to escape. For the first time I realised how much we had in common. She is blessed with my fortitude. Wordlessly I made her understand that now was not the time to escape. My wife and son were too sick. Before very long the men wanted us to continue. They forced us back into the machine even though we made it clear we did not want to go. This sequence of events repeated itself several times until we reached our destination. By this time we were all very weak. I was greatly relieved as neither I nor my family had any intention of spending one moment longer in their contraption.

At the village the men separated us. They washed me with water. We never use water to wash. It is too precious a commodity. We only use

smoke. They also scrubbed me with a foaming substance. It tasted terrible and stung my eyes. I found
it all very humiliating. They washed me many times,
five in all, until my skin was raw. Each time they
passed a machine over me that clicked loudly. They
only stopped washing me when the clicking ceased.

My wife in particular was very afraid. She is not
permitted to bathe with strangers. The penalties for
doing this are severe. She told me that she saw another woman like her while they were bathing her.
The men assured me that this was not so. They told
me that in fact she had seen her own reflection in a
thing called a mirror. Later I tried explaining this to
her but she was not convinced. I didn't completely
understand it myself. The only time I have seen my
reflection is in a pool of water, and to my
knowledge water does not adhere to walls. Eventually, because of her stern protests, they decided to
respect her wishes and she was not washed as I
was.

I was further concerned for her once they had
told me that we had interfered with a white man's
ceremony. In my culture a women is not allowed to
see the business of men and if she does the punishment can be death. However, they convinced me
that she would not be punished and we would be

safe as long as we never again travelled through that area.

After a few days they took us in their terrible machines to another village of theirs called Yalata. It took a great deal of time to reach there. However our ordeal was not over. The first thing they did was shoot my dogs. I cannot begin to explain the rage I felt when they did this. After that they prevented us from leaving. On one occasion they inserted some very small spears in me and took away some of my blood.

One or two seasons passed and I longed to see my homeland again. A sadness completely took over me. Still they would not let us go. Gradually I became very ill. Things grew on my skin and I began to lose my sight. I now fear that I do not have much time left in this world. I miss my wife and children. They no longer let me see them. I hope that the time will soon come when at the very least my spirit can go home. I no longer wish to be a prisoner of the invader.

THREE

....

ALICE SPRINGS

THE DEALER

They had been cruising along the highway for about half an hour when Rob abruptly jumped on the brakes and brought the car to a virtual standstill. They were all catapulted forward out of their seats. Billy managed to brace himself on the front seat and barely avoided being launched into the windscreen. Tex slapped both hands on the dashboard to prevent himself from suffering the same fate.

'Whoa!'

'Sorry, nearly missed the turnoff.'

He pulled off the main road and onto an un-marked side road.

'Just got to pick someth'n up.'

'Um, ok.'

Billy realised it was in his own best interests to seriously take into account Rob's erratic driving. He searched for a seatbelt without success. Looking around the backseat the only thing that seemed to offer a secure anchor was the armrest on the door. He took hold of it with a firm grip and kept an eye on the road ahead. The storm clouds still hung in the sky in front of them. They had remained static for some time. It was as if the mountain range had stopped them in their tracks and they needed to further build up strength to breech and flow over them. As they drove down the side road and towards the clouds they grew steadily in stature.

He was intrigued by Tex's guitar abilities and, even though he was competing with the din of the engine and the cassette player, decided to make conversation. The tape seemed to speed up and slow down, not unlike Rob's driving. It distorted the music. Billy had encountered similar problems himself and assumed the tape had stretched after spending a good deal of its life baking on the dashboard of the car. The music was unfamiliar to Billy, an odd mix of reggae and rock. He asked Rob to turn it up.

'Who's this?' Billy struggled to make himself heard over the music and roar of the engine. Rob turned down the music.

'Coloured Stone, song called Black Boy.'

'They're not bad. Where are they from?'

'Down south, 'round Ceduna. They've played up here before, though. They've been around for a while.'

'Ceduna? My mum was from around there, I think.'

'Really?'

'Yeah, but I don't know much about her. She died when I was pretty young.' 'Sorry to hear that. Do you know where her people were from?'

'People?'

'Yeah, her tribe.'

Billy had never considered the question of his Aboriginality, let alone that he was from a tribe. His father had been a low-paid dockside labourer and they had not had a lot of contact with Aboriginal people, even though he had grown up in a town where the white population was in the minority. He could barely remember his mother and only knew that she had died after a long illness. His father had told him very little about her. It was a subject he had always avoided discussing. He did know she had Aboriginal ancestry but had no idea to what extent. He only knew that she had succumbed to cancer when she was still quite young.

'Nope, my father brought me up and didn't tell me much about her. He didn't like to talk about her. Guess the memory was too painful.'

'That's a shame. Well, she could have come from one of a few tribes. A lot of folks got moved down to the coast during the British nuclear tests. Who knows, you could even be related to us.'

This last comment surprised Billy. It hadn't occurred to him that he could have a wider family. His father had been a bit of a loner. They had kept to themselves and he had never had any contact with his relatives. The subject was starting to distress him. He wished he knew more. He regretted that he had not made more effort to ask his father about his heritage. He shifted the conversation.

'So where'd you learn to play guitar, Tex?' 'Just picked it up.'

'Played in any bands?'

'Na, not really.'

Rob thumped him hard on the shoulder.

'He's lying to you. Played in quite a good one for a while. Doesn't like to talk about it though.'

Billy was intrigued. 'So who were they?'

Tex didn't respond. After an uneasy pause Rob spoke up on his behalf. 'Let's just say it all got a bit serious and they wanted him to move to the big smoke, the city. He went down one time and didn't like it. Lucky for us, I say. At least we get to enjoy his playing, eh mate?'

Tex remained noncommittal but seemed to lighten up a little and a sly grin spread across his face.

Rob slowed the car and scanned the trees at the side of the road.

'Nearly there.'

He brought the vehicle gingerly to a stop. This time he made sure not to jolt his passengers. He then turned the car onto a narrow dirt track. Struggling with the heavy steering wheel and gunning the engine he launched the car up over a mound of sand on the verge of the road. He then skilfully manoeuvred it between the trees. Billy couldn't even see a road and was convinced they would get bogged in the soft sand. However, clearly Rob was a capable driver in this kind of terrain. After a short journey they came to an opening in the trees. Under an enormous ghost gum was a ramshackle caravan. Its wheels had been removed and it sat on cinder blocks which were almost completely submerged in the sand. The place seemed deserted. Apart from the caravan there was very little to speak of in the immediate vicinity, except for the remnants of an open fire.

They got out of the car. Billy stood up straight and stretched. With his hands on his hips he arched his back, looking skywards. The dark storm clouds now hung directly above, holding their position. It seemed as if they were waiting patiently for a signal before unleashing their fury. Billy tried to get a sense of his surroundings but the trees and scrub blocked all views beyond the small clearing. He couldn't even see the mountain range they had been previously driving towards. They seemed perfectly hidden. Even the caravan blended into the bush, coated as it was in a layer of dust.

Rob and Tex approached the caravan and Rob rapped his knuckles on the screen door. The inside door opened and a figure pushed the screen door aside. The interior was so dark that Billy could only make out a shadow. Rob stretched out a hand and it was heartily shaken by the figure inside. Rob motioned Billy over. Standing in the doorway was a very skinny white man, with red hair and a scraggly beard. He seemed surprised to see Billy, and a look of unease flashed across his face. Rob murmured something to him and his apprehension seemed to abate. They all stepped inside. The interior of the caravan was cramped, filled with all manner of junk. Billy could make out a small kitchen filled with dirty dishes. In what appeared to be a living room was an old couch and two reclining chairs, with a low coffee table as its centrepiece. The man stepped over the clutter and cleared some space on the well-worn couch. They all looked for somewhere to sit. Billy found a chair under a box and moved it to one side. Rob introduced the man. 'This is Ron.'

Ron nodded at him and Billy reciprocated. He then took on the guise of a shopkeeper. 'So what'll it be today?'

He looked past Billy and indicated to someone that they should leave. Billy turned to see a small woman standing in the shadows. She dutifully obeyed and stepped out of the caravan. Billy heard the screen door clatter as she swept it shut behind her.

'Just a small bag,' said Rob.

Ron directed his attention to Billy, 'You want someth'n?'

Billy didn't know what that something was and shook his head.

'Ok, no worries.'

Ron reached under the couch and produced a large Arnott's biscuit tin. He put it on the table in front of him and pried open the lid with his finger-nails. They were nicotine stained, and there was so much dirt under them that it looked as if Ron had been walking on his hands through the desert. The tin was filled to the brim with small bags of marijuana. He laid three of them in a neat row on the table. 'Take your pick.'

Rob scooped up the centre one, stretched out one leg and fumbled in his front pocket, pulling out a crisp, twenty-dollar note. He passed it to Ron who redeposited the other bags in the tin and sealed it.

'You guys want one on me?'

Tex and Rob nodded in acknowledgement. Billy wasn't a regular dope smoker but had friends that were. He had the occasional smoke when out with them. Invariably this occurred when he had already had too much to drink. As a result it usually didn't sit well with him. However, feeling decidedly sober and not wanting to offend his companions, he felt obliged to accept the offer. Ron reached around the side of the couch and produced a large Coca-Cola bottle, which had been expertly fabricated into a water pipe. It had already been prepared for the occasion, and the makeshift pipe protruding out from the bottle's midriff was filled to the brim. He brought the mouthpiece up to his lips and lit the contents with an enormous, pink, plastic cigarette lighter. The water in the bottle gurgled loudly and he drew the smoke in deeply. He then passed the bottle across to Billy amid a grey cloud of exhaled smoke.

'Visitors first.'

Billy took a deep breath and then let it out. He leant over the pipe and drew in a large mouthful of smoke. His eyes bulged as he tried to hold it in. He spluttered and choked. He only just managed to place the pipe on the coffee table before doubling over in an uncontrollable fit of coughing. The three other men erupted in an explosion of laughter. Billy ignored them, trying in vain to stop the coughing, and writhing painfully in his seat.

Ron pushed a dirty glass filled with tepid water across the table towards him. 'Here, have some of this.'

Billy regained his composure somewhat and reached for the glass. He gulped down a large mouthful. Tears streamed down his face and he wiped them away with the back of his sleeve. The pipe proceeded around the group, all of them chuckling heartily. When it made its way back to Billy he refused. 'Think I'll be all right, thanks.'

They all smiled broadly at him. The water pipe did another circuit, after which its contents were exhausted. It then became the centrepiece on the table. All three men sank back into their seats wearing satisfied looks. It was deathly still. Billy could hear the faint ticking of a clock somewhere in the dark recesses of the caravan. Apart from that he could only hear his own blood rushing past his ears. The sound grew steadily in volume. He felt uneasy and guessed the drug was doing its job. He took another slow sip of water before settling back in his chair and joining the other men in studying the table decoration.

After what seemed an eternity, Rob broke the silence. 'Think we're gonna make a move.'

Ron nodded. 'I'll see you out.'

They all stood up simultaneously and waited for Billy, who was slow to react. He was firmly ensconced in his chair and had trouble getting to his feet. When he had raised himself to his full height he felt dizzy and it took him a moment to steady himself. 'Ok, let's go.'

Rob waited for Ron to move past him and followed him to the door. Ron kicked the screen door open and it clattered on the aluminium wall of the caravan, before swinging back and nearly hitting him in the face. Billy could hear the sound reverberating off the nearby hills. They stepped outside into the waning light. The sun had begun to set. Billy looked towards the horizon, which was painted a bright pink, graduating to a deep purple over his head. He marvelled at its beauty. He peered out into the half-light and wondered where Ron's girlfriend could have gone, before noticing a slight figure bent over a small campfire. She looked like a child with the glow of the fire dancing over her shoulders and framing her in silhouette. He stood transfixed for a while, watching the flames. The others began bidding farewell to Ron. Rob called out to him and snapped him out of his daze. He turned reluctantly away from the fire and wandered over to the car.

'See you 'round,' said Ron.

Billy severely doubted this but replied with a smile, 'Yeah, see you 'round.' They all climbed into the vehicle. After a few failed attempts Rob succeeded in starting the car. He revved the engine vigorously to make sure it would keep running. 'Think I need to get her tuned.'

He slowly turned the vehicle around in the small clearing. They all waved at Ron and Billy's gaze settled on the fire. It mesmerised him once again. Peering through his window he followed its light. He turned in his seat to get a better look through the rear window as they pulled away from the clearing. A large hump in the road sent him crashing into the side door. He gently rubbed his shoulder. It reminded him of his secret oath to remain vigilant whilst in Rob's car. The back seat was almost becoming a second home. He seemed to have spent more time there than anywhere else. He had gradually made more room for his feet after systematically shifting most of the rubbish to the opposing floor well. He stretched out his legs and settled back into his seat. Looking skywards through his window he noted that there were no stars yet where the sky was clear. The storm clouds were still blocking a great deal of his view of the heavens. He wondered if they would ever break or if the clouds would just clear without bringing any welcome moisture. The smoke had slowed his senses and he chose to be blissfully unaware of the conversation going on in the front seat. A smile spread across his face and then quickly melted as the car leapt over another particularly large mound. It lifted him completely up off his seat and he banged his forehead against an unpadded part of the ceiling. He cursed and rubbed the pain away with the palm of one hand, while gripping the armrest tightly with the other. Much to his relief it was the last bump before they turned back onto the relatively smooth main dirt road.

Rob guided the car into the middle of the road and planted his foot heavily on the accelerator. The back of the vehicle fish-tailed and its wheels spun before finding traction. It swerved sideways across the road before straightening out. Billy felt as if he was being launched into space, with the world outside descending quickly into an impenetrable, inky blackness. The only light inside the car now came from the glow of the dashboard illuminating the occupants of the front seat. They seemed larger than normal and he felt small and distant, pinned as he was to the back of his seat. He felt a surge of panic before reminding himself that he was under the influence of the drug. His heartbeat slowed and he closed his eyes, trying to concentrate on something familiar. His girlfriend. He had to call his girlfriend. 'First thing I'm gonna do when I get to the town.'

'Wha?'

'Oh, sorry, nothing; just talking to myself.'

Billy was grateful that he was shrouded in darkness and that Rob couldn't see the flush of embarrassment on his cheeks.

'Betta keep tabs on that, mate. You know what they say 'bout talking to yourself?'

'Yeah.'

He felt a lump in his shirt pocket and was overjoyed to find another Mars Bar. The pangs of hunger were making themselves known once again. They vocalised their presence through the loud gurgling of his stomach. It took a few moments to extract the chocolate bar from its wrapper, as it had melted in its packaging. Having pulled it free he tossed the wrapper on the pile of rubbish at his feet. He wolfed it down, self-conscious that he hadn't offered any to Rob or Tex. He decided he was due for a decent meal and made a mental note to add that to his agenda for the evening. As the car sped down the road Billy hoped it wouldn't take too long to reach their destination.

THE CASINO

Billy was confounded. Here he was somewhere out in the desert, miles from anywhere, in the epicentre of nowhere, and he was being barred entrance because of a dress code. Surely the casino needed all the clientele it could lay its hands on. He looked up at a sign on the wall. It spelt out in bold, block letters:

DRESS CODE:
No thongs, no jeans, no collarless shirts.
WE RESERVE THE RIGHT TO REFUSE
SERVICE TO ANYONE.

He was wearing torn jeans and his sneakers were a bit dusty, but they were both new. He wore a shirt with a collar. It was a flannelette shirt and needed a wash, but it was also in pretty good condition. He thought he looked quite fashionable; holey jeans were all the rage. After all, he wasn't a brick-layer by profession. A security man the size of a medium-sized family car had stopped him at the entrance and he had been separated from Rob and Tex. He stood in the foyer feeling somewhat ex-posed. There were lights everywhere. He could hear the tinkling of poker machines clanging away every time someone walked in or out through the sliding automatic doors to the main room.

The place was not as appealing as he had first thought. He had been happy to arrive at what ap-peared to be a bastion of western civilisation. How-ever, the short time he had spent in the wide open spaces had changed his attitude. He now felt hemmed in and not at all comfortable.

Rob had said they were going there to play a bit of poker, but Billy really wasn't that interested. In the first place, he was terrible at the game and knew he would lose. It occurred to him that being barred from the place was a blessing in disguise. He would walk out of there with empty pockets if he stayed. Once inside he would get caught up in the whole thing and squander what little he had. He had al-ready had enough surprises, and didn't want to wake up the next day totally destitute.

Rob and Tex had already entered the club, so Billy felt as if he had lost his only lifeline. He considered his options. His head was still a little clouded from the marijuana but it was slowly clearing. He fought to get his thinking straight. To his relief Rob came back out of the casino. He was evidently looking for Billy and spotted him standing forlornly, alone in the centre of the foyer.

'What's going on?'

'They won't let me in.'

Rob screwed up his face in a mixture of surprise and bewilderment. Billy indicated the sign on the wall and in a deadpan voice, filled with sarcasm, said, 'It seems I don't come up to their standards.'

'You gotta be kiddin'.'

Rob took a moment to think. He scrutinised Billy's attire and then looked down at himself. Billy noticed for the first time that Rob was actually quite smartly dressed. Even his boots were polished.

'Think I've probably got some clothes for you in the car.'

'It's ok. Don't think I want to go in there anyway.'

'Ah, c'mon, no probs.'

Abruptly Rob walked off towards the parking lot and his car. Billy followed reluctantly. At the car,

Rob cracked open the boot and fumbled around inside. The distant street lighting made it hard to see anything, but the interior of the luggage space was coated in fine, red dust. Rob found what he was looking for and pulled out an old sports training bag. He slapped it a few times and a cloud of dust arose. They stood back to avoid it. Rob dumped the bag on the ground and another cloud of dust rose. He bent down, unzipped it and pulled out a pair of pants and a shirt. They didn't look as though they would fit.

'Think I've got a pair of boots in here somewhere.'

'Look, Rob, don't worry, mate. I'll wait out here. Not really into casinos anyway.'

Rob looked hurt.

'It's no big deal. We'll sort it out. C'mon, it'll be fun.'

'Na, don't think it would be such a good idea. Don't have a lot of cash anyway.'

'You won't need it. We'll look after you.'

'No, it's ok, really. I'll just hang out here.'

Rob could see he wasn't going to persuade Billy to change his mind. He stuffed everything back into the bag, zipped it up and, after dropping it in the boot, slammed the door shut. They both jumped out of the way of the rising pall of dust. Rob pulled his shirt away from his chest and shook off as much of the stuff as he could.

'You sure? Last chance.'

'Really, it's ok.'

'Ok, suit yerself.'

They walked slowly back to the entrance of the casino and into the foyer. The bright lights and tinkling machines engulfed them once more. It was like stepping into a different world.

'I'll catch up with you later.'

'No worries. Think I'll just have a wander around.'

'Ok. We can crash later at a friend's place. Car's open if you need anything.'

'Thanks.'

Rob walked back into the casino and was swallowed up by a cacophony of noise and flashing lights. Billy watched him go and then turned towards the door. Next to the main entrance was a yellow payphone, bolted to the wall. He hadn't noticed it before. He had also completely forgotten the main purpose of travelling to town with Rob. He still had to sort things out with his wife-to-be.

Elizabeth, or Beth for short. That wasn't the only thing that was short about her. There was her diminutive stature; and then there was her quick temper. He had a very real and palpable fear of it.

She could just go off. He had no defence against it. He could stand up for himself, but with her it was a different matter. Even the night out had to be negotiated in detail to forestall her wrath. He felt hemmed in by her. She was too controlling. He couldn't be entirely himself. He questioned if she was worth it. He used to think so. She could be the kindest person in the world. Once they had been inseparable and he was certain she was the one. Recently that had changed. He didn't know what it was. Maybe it was the pressure of the whole marriage thing. Deep down he knew it wasn't only that. He had doubts.

It dawned on him that he hadn't even considered what he was going to say to her. It was going to require an enormous amount of tact. More than he possessed. He weighed up the situation. He was too late for the wedding, of that he was sure. She would not be in the mood for excuses. The whole idea of talking to her was daunting. Maybe she wasn't even home. He needed time to think. As he was already late it wouldn't matter if he waited a bit longer. The damage had already been done.

The brightly coloured phone seemed to be calling him over and urging him to face up to his responsibilities. He couldn't do it. He needed fresh air. The whole place was stifling. With all the noise and lights the room was closing in around him. He pulled his eyes away from the phone. Its colour yelled coward at him. He made a snap decision to make the call in the morning. He couldn't do it now. He had to get outside.

Billy practically ran out the entrance. He was barely outside when he collided with Mabel. She had her head down and was fumbling in her purse.

'Oops, sorry.'

He shook his head. 'My mistake,' he said.

'Hey, saw you today in the store. Billy wasn't it?'

'Yep.'

'Where you off too?'

Billy took a moment to catch his breath. 'Dunno. Not in there, anyway. They wouldn't let me in.'

'Really?'

'Bad dress sense, according to them.'

'Aah.'

Mabel was clearly aware of the need to dress up for the place. On appraising her attire and make-up he concluded that she had gone above and beyond what was required. She looked fantastic.

'Yeah, they're a bit picky around here. I was on my way to meet some girlfriends but they've piked. I thought, seeing that I was already here, I might as well have a quick look. But if you like we can go somewhere else?'

Billy was taken aback. It surprised him how everyone he met here was more than willing to drop everything and spend time with him. He was also aware of Rob's feeling for her and was reluctant to step on his territory. She sensed his reservations and put them to rest.

'It's not a date,' she said flatly.

'Oh no, of course not,' he replied sheepishly.

Billy was reassured, but still found it difficult to relate to her forwardness. Everyone was extremely open and friendly. It was something he couldn't quite come to terms with.

'Got a car over here. Don't come into town much, but maybe we can just go for a drink somewhere.'

Billy was grateful for the chance to put some distance between him and the telephone. It could wait.

'Ok, you lead the way.'

As they walked across the parking lot thunder growled ominously in the distance and echoed off the surrounding hills. The rain still hadn't come, but it couldn't be far off. He could now feel moisture hanging in the air. Billy was certain that when it finally did arrive the heavens would truly open.

LINE DANCING

Not much time had passed since Billy had been in a public bar, but it felt like ages. Even though he had been a frequent visitor to such establishments, it seemed a strange environment after spending time in the community. As he and Mabel walked in they were confronted with an enormous bar. It stood at the far end of a large room and stretched along one wall. The rest of the cavernous room was remarkably sparse except for a scattering of tables and chairs. The bar itself took on the appearance of an island, well lit, warm and cosy, whereas the rest of the room was dimly lit, cold and uninviting. As they walked across the room towards the bar they passed a group of people dressed in cowboy clothing. Some were wearing Stetsons. About twenty of them sat together at a long table. They were huddled in deep conversation over their drinks.

Mabel and Billy each pulled a stool up to the bar. The bar itself was very solid, constructed entirely of old, jarrah railway sleepers, sanded and polished to a high gloss. It was massive, thick and unyielding, but the colour of the wood made it appear soft and malleable, almost like clay. Seated at one end of the bar was a lone, long-haired Aboriginal man wearing a heavy jacket and quietly sipping a beer. He barely acknowledged their presence. The bartender, a man in his late forties, very tall and built as solidly as the bar, asked what they wanted to drink. They both ordered beer and, for a moment, stared at their own reflections in the long mirror behind the bar.

Mabel broke the silence. 'So, what brings you up this way? You're from Adelaide, aren't you?'

'Yeah, this is a bit out of the way for me.' Billy took a long look at Mabel and decided he could confide in her. 'It's a bit embarrassing, really. I was out with my mates and had a bit too much to drink. From what I can work out they stuffed me in a bus and I woke to find myself here. Well, not actually here. Rob kind of found me wandering around out on the highway. I guess you know the rest.'

In fact, the rest was so much more, but Billy really didn't want to go into it. He was just getting to know Mabel and it didn't feel right to burden her with all his problems.

'Yeah, he told me he nearly ran you over and that you seemed a bit lost.'

'Lost doesn't even begin to sum up my predicament.'

Their conversation was interrupted by the bartender arriving with their drinks. The glasses were extremely well chilled. Icy vapour rose from them.

'I'll get these if you like?'

Billy, who was painfully aware of his financial situation, responded with a grateful 'Thanks.'

'So what are your plans?'

'Finding a way home is pretty high on the agenda. Think I'll make some calls in the morning then head home. Not really sure what I should do around here anyway. None of this was planned, you know.'

Mabel appeared to consider this for a moment. 'What's the big hurry? I mean, you're here now. You might as well have a look around. I'm sure if you wanted to hang around for a few days someone'd put you up.'

Billy was unconvinced. 'I'll have a think about it.'

He swung around on his barstool and surveyed the rest of the room. Behind them the patrons at the long table were standing up and had started moving some of the furniture against a far wall. The bartender, leaning on the bar behind them, enquired if everything was to their liking.

Billy turned to face him. 'We're fine, thanks. What's going on?'

'Oh, it's the weekly line dancing meeting.'

'Line dancing?' Billy chuckled to himself. He didn't even know that this sort of thing went on in Australia. He thought it only happened in America. It reinforced his impression that he had found himself in the Wild West. One of the line dancers, a woman in her early forties, who was decked out in full country-and-western regalia, stomped up to the bar and began chatting with the barman. He made some adjustments to the control panel of a sound system mounted on the back wall. When he flipped a few switches on another panel next to it, the lighting in the room changed dramatically. The place was transformed into a kind of disco. Small, multicoloured lights on the ceiling flashed on and off in an irregular pattern. In the centre of the room a miniature mirror ball twirled above the dance floor. The woman peered intently at another console at the far end of the bar and hit a button. Country music erupted at high volume from speakers suspended above the bar. Billy Ray Cyrus began crooning about his achy breaky heart.

As the chorus kicked in Billy groaned. The song had been playing on high rotation on radio at home, and he found it profoundly irritating. He and Mabel took one look at each other and slid further up the bar, away from the din. They sat next to the lone man who was still engrossed in his beer. Mabel seemed to know him but avoided looking at him. She half turned away from him and Billy and watched the dancers. They had formed into three neat, parallel lines and were slapping their heels in time to the music.

Billy ignored them. He turned to the man and asked where he was from. He mumbled back over his glass. 'Hermannsburg.'

The name was familiar to Billy but he couldn't quite place it.

The man noticed his confusion. 'It's where Albert Namatjira's from. He was my uncle, by the way.'

'Wow, really?'

Billy knew a little about Albert Namatjira, mainly because when he was a child one of his prints had hung on his bedroom wall. He had seen a similar print on the wall of the hut he had stayed in at the community. Although he didn't know much about the painter, he knew he had been widely respected for his striking artwork.

'Had to show a film crew 'round out there to-day.'

'Oh yeah? What were they doing?'

'Mak'n a documentary 'bout my uncle.'

The man seemed reasonably friendly so Billy asked him if he wanted a drink. He acknowledged with a slight nod. Billy relaxed and decided to stretch his self-imposed budget. He felt like something stronger.

'Would you like a whiskey?'

'Ok.'

'And how about you, Mabel?'

Mabel was still engrossed in the line dancers and took a moment to respond. 'Huh? Oh, no thanks. I'll just have a beer.'

Billy waved the barman over and ordered a beer and two whiskeys. Mabel quietly accepted her drink and continued watching the line dancers. Billy raised his glass to the man who returned the gesture. He downed his whiskey in one go and then moved back to his beer. Billy sipped thoughtfully on his. 'So, are you a bit of a guide then?'

'No, not really. I just know a bit about my uncle and those people wanted a bit of info.'

'I'm kind of new up here myself. Maybe you could show me around a bit?'

The man was noncommittal. 'Maybe.'

'Must be kinda cool being related to Albert Namatjira. Did you know him well?'

The man didn't react for a time and stared blankly at his drink. Slowly his body language changed and he appeared to stiffen. When he replied his tone had changed dramatically. 'You know what? You people are all the same. You come up here and think you can just take whatever you like. You get what you want and then leave, and what do we see for it?'

Billy was surprised by his sudden irritation. He hadn't intended to insult the man and wasn't quite sure what he had done to warrant his reaction. 'I think you got me wrong. I don't want anything from you. Was just trying to have a chat.'

The man seemed to be caught up in his own thoughts and ignored Billy's response. 'As far as I'm concerned you can all go to hell. We just wanna be left alone.'

Billy was slightly taken aback but could see that he had touched a nerve. He let the man be and turned to Mabel. Abruptly, the man pushed himself away from the bar and stood up. He walked behind Billy, who assumed he was on his way to the toilet. Suddenly the man grabbed Billy by the hair and drove his head violently down onto the leading edge of the bar, splitting his forehead open in the process. Billy reacted quickly, bringing his hands up onto the bar, locking his elbows and bracing himself as the man attempted to repeat the manoeuvre. The big barman flew into action with surprising agility. He lunged over the bar and seized the man's hand. A long struggle ensued, the two men fighting over possession of Billy's head. His neck was wrenched about. He felt like a rag doll, at the mercy of the two men. His mind swam, and blood seeped from his open forehead and ran down his face. It felt as if his hair was being ripped from his skull. In the middle of all this a curious thought crossed his mind: he made a mental note to get his hair cut short at the next opportunity.

His eyes wandered over the wall behind the barman and settled on a dusty placard. It was nicotine stained and had turned a deep yellow from the cigarette smoke. It read: 'You're never more alive than when you think you're going to die.' Thanks for the poignant observation, he thought to himself.

He turned his attention to the mirror, stretching along the wall. In its reflection he thought he could see the man's aggression beginning to subside. He could hear the barman talking softly to him and encouraging him to relax. In the shadows behind his assailant he could just make out a figure standing against the far wall. The disco lights flickered over him, creating strange shadows on his face and glinting off his cloak. A cloak made entirely of feathers. Billy felt drawn into the mirror and his eyes locked with those of Pidgin. His piercing, blue-green eyes dominated everything, and the rest of the room went out of focus. There was only Pidgin. A calm come over Billy and he relaxed his grip on the bar. His attacker and the barman followed suit. They cautiously release his head. The barman walked quickly around the bar and guided the man to a stool further down. Billy felt a hand on his shoulder and realised it was Mabel. He was dazed and had completely forgotten that she was also there. She grabbed a towel which was lying on the bar and pressed it to his forehead.

'C'mon, let's get you cleaned up.'

She helped him to his feet and led him away by the hand. He looked at her hand in his. She had very well manicured nails. He felt faint and followed her lead like a dutiful child. She took him into the ladies' toilet and sat him down in one of the cubicles. She then proceeded to wet the towel and clean his face. She gently daubed the wound and inspected the damage. There was a lot of blood but the cut was fairly superficial.

'Looks like you'll live,' she said jokingly, 'but y'r gonna have one hell of a headache tomorrow.'

Billy could already feel the bump on his fore-head swelling up. He didn't feel well at all and fought to prevent himself from throwing up the meagre contents of his stomach. The same woman he'd seen earlier in the line dancing group walked into the toilet and surveyed the situation. She first looked down at Billy and then turned her attention to Mabel. 'I think you'd better leave.'

Mabel nodded tentatively in agreement. Content that her directions would be followed, the woman left the room. Billy was confused. Why should they leave? He hadn't been the aggressor. He hadn't pro-voked a fight. It then dawned on him that he was the outsider and as such probably had fewer rights than his attacker. Still, it didn't seem right. Mabel carefully scrutinised his head again. She folded the towel and pressed it to his forehead, telling him to hold it in place. She seemed satisfied that they could move and helped him to his feet.

'Let's get out o' here.'

He nodded meekly, and together they walked out of the toilet. They crossed the room, skirting the dance floor. Billy peered out from under his makeshift bandage. The man was sitting quietly at the bar, staring once again into his beer glass. The barman was leaning against the freezers, keeping a watchful eye on him. No one seemed to be paying any attention at all to them. The dancers were in full stride, energetically stomping out a pattern in unison. The disco lighting flashed and panned over the whole bar. The music was unrelenting.

They slipped out of the front door and found themselves standing in torrential rain. They were instantly saturated. Billy let the rain pour over him. It was so intense that it immediately started to seep into his shoes. He removed the bandage from his injury and turned his head skywards. The rain played on his face. Great, heavy drops stung him as they hit his skin. He breathed deeply and took a moment to compose himself. He could taste salty, watered-down blood in mouth. He wiped his face with the towel before pressing it once again to his throbbing forehead.

Mabel laid a hand on his shoulder. 'Let's get out o' this.'

'Ok.'

More than anything in the world, that was exactly what he wanted: not to be where he was right now. She suggested he should stay at Doug's house for the night. It was only a short walk from there. He was feeling miserable, soaked to the skin and willing to comply with anything. Together they walked down the street without saying another word. The rain pounded down even harder. It enveloped them in a cacophony of white noise. Not unlike the sound of static on an empty television channel.

DOUG AND PIDGIN

Billy sat bolt upright in bed. A strange bed. Accustomed as he now was to waking up in unusual surroundings, this time it was different. He was in mortal fear for his life. The room was unfamiliar. It was dark and he could barely see anything. The only light came from a crack under a door at the foot of his bed. He thought he heard loud noises outside. He was sure someone was banging at a window to his right and trying to get in. He felt as if he was under attack. Yet the room itself was empty. Or was it? His eyes began to adjust to the meagre light. Slowly he made out forms in the room. He saw shadows everywhere and one in particular caught his attention. There was a giant bird perched on a dresser against the wall and next to the door. He screamed. The bird raised its head from within its plumage. It was the head of a man, an old man, with eyes that cut through him. Billy struggled to breathe. With considerable effort he filled his lungs and let out another piercing scream. There was the sound of heavy footsteps outside the bedroom door before it swung open and bright light streamed in. Another shadow entered. This one was, indeed, in the shape of a man. A large man. He stood silhouetted in the doorway.

'Billy, it's ok mate. It's Doug.'

Billy's mind raced.

Doug?

Doug who?

Was he someone he could trust?

He knew a Doug.

Doug was the old guy on the steps in front of the store talking to the kids.

Doug was ok.

Doug was indeed someone he could trust.

Billy managed to calm himself somewhat. He raised one arm feebly and pointed towards the figure on the dresser. Doug wheeled around. He stood only about a metre from the cupboard. Doug took half a step backwards before letting his shoulders slump. He seemed to relax, and the atmosphere in the whole room seemed to do the same.

Doug began speaking to the figure on the dresser in soft but forceful tones. The bird man cocked his head to one side and listened intently to Doug. He trained his ears on the conversation, trying desperately to hear what was being said. It was impossible. Doug spoke slowly and in a low voice, almost a murmur. The conversation was entirely one way. Pidgin occasionally responded with a barely perceptible nod. Then his head cocked this way and that with very sharp, birdlike movements.

Billy tentatively reached up to his pounding forehead. It was very swollen. He could feel textile covering his skin and the pull of a wide plaster, stuck above his eyebrow. The events of the evening came flooding back and he realised he must be suffering from some form of shock. After all, he had received a pretty decent bump to his head. It became clear to him that he wasn't under attack, although the unsettling feeling continued to bubble in his subconscious.

Doug continued talking to Pidgin for some time and when he was finished he turned to face Billy.

'This is your guardian, Billy. He's here to protect you. You musn't be afraid of him. He was very concerned about you. He's here to watch over you. He'll appear in times of trouble or when he senses that trouble will arise. You must trust him. He looked over your father and your grandfather and all those who have gone before. He knows more than you or I will ever know.'

Doug turned to Pidgin and reassured him that everything was in order. Pidgin seemed to accept this and settled. He lifted his shoulders and his coat of feathers half engulfed his head. Doug stepped in front of Pidgin and into Billy's line of sight.

'Now it's time you rested. You've had quite a night. Probably gonna wake up later with a bit of a headache. You're safe here; no one's gonna hurt you. Tomorrow we'll talk some more. For now it's better if you get a decent sleep. I'll see you in the morning.'

Billy nodded silently, turned slowly onto his side and pulled the sheets up to his earlobes. He could sense the two figures staring at him and felt their concern. It had been a lot to take in, but he was no longer racked by fear. He felt safe and secure. He let himself slip away into what would become a dreamless slumber. He barely heard the click of the bedroom door shutting as Doug walked past the empty dresser and left the room.

....

Outside, the heavens had truly opened and the storm raged on. The iron roof of Doug's house roared in protest. The sound was deafening, such was the deluge. Dry riverbeds flowed again and swelled up, breaking their banks. Dirt roads became impassable and were washed away. The hard-baked floor of the desert refused to let the water seep through. It was like concrete. The water sat on top of it and spread out in all directions, turning once parched plateaus into enormous lakes. Up in the hills, rocky outcrops were washed clean and torrents of water flowed hastily into waterholes. It filled them to the brim. By morning the rain subsided and stopped. The landscape had been transformed. As dawn broke, birds of all descriptions came to life. They sang and chirped and played happily in their new surroundings.

OOLDEA RAILWAY SIDING

....

1932

I spotted her in the crowd and immediately felt sick to the pit of my stomach. In retrospect I guess it was love at first sight. My first wife had never made me feel this way. I had recently lost her to a new and strange disease which was yet another by-product of the invaders. Before they came such things did not exist. She hadn't been the only one to suffer. A great many had succumbed to this illness. This came about with the arrival of their spirit men. They didn't respect our stories. They tried to teach us new ones. Their stories were from another land. They didn't have relevance here. They spoke of one, all-seeing spirit. For us there are many. Everything we see—every rock and tree and animal— they all have names and they all have stories. The invaders should understand this. We do not force our knowledge upon them, yet they do this to us.

We can see our spirits by the traces they have left. I cannot see their spirit.

For a while we accepted their stories and what we thought was their assistance. Because of this my wife is no longer here. I have had to wipe her name from my memory. She became ill from their food and the hidden things they brought with them. Many of our tribe passed into the spirit world because of this. I can still see their bodies laid out in rows upon the ground and covered in some kind of white material. At the time I fled in fear, as did many of my tribesmen. The fear saved us, though, and because of it we are still walking in this world.

In any case, upon meeting this girl I felt driven to find out more about her. I took this feeling as a sign that my time of mourning was over and that I could stop wearing the white ochre.

I didn't know which skin she was but I felt relatively safe to pursue and court her as she wasn't from my immediate family. My greatest fear was that she was from a hostile tribe and they wouldn't be willing to trade her. I didn't have much of value to trade and was apprehensive that I would have an uphill battle trying to persuade her people to let her go with me. I could have asked my own relatives to help out but I didn't want to impose on them. Things were hard enough as they were. It had become more and more difficult to find things of quality to trade. The invaders had expanded their stranglehold on our land and we could no longer go to many of our traditional sources. The most prized ochre was to be found in the mine at Bookatoo. But the area had been taken over by the invaders and it had become too dangerous to go there. The Dieri had also been driven from their lands and could no longer grow and harvest pituri. Of course, there were other sources for these things but they were substandard. Unfortunately, now we were faced with no other alternative and reduced to making do with what we still had. It was a sorry situation.

Having nothing else of value to trade, I would have to rely on my spear-making abilities. My father had taught me well and I had unlocked the secret to getting the weight and balance right. I was confident that my handiwork was worth something. Not everyone could make weapons of such quality. They were so sleek and incredibly accurate. I was proud of my skills. I had speared many a kangaroo from a great distance and had excellent success with smaller animals. I could only hope they would be of sufficient quality and prized enough to trade for a wife.

We had been travelling our usual route along the water lines towards the great salt lake when I had encountered her. On our journey we were shocked to see how much had changed. What had happened at the place where I found her was even more disturbing. My forefathers had always gathered at one particular waterhole. I had never travelled so far but had been taught how to find it and had its position engraved on my woomera. It was a soak of immense purity and went down into the deepest recesses of the earth. The elders believed it would never run dry, not even in the driest of seasons. In the end they were wrong. Even they could not predict the changes that were happening to our land. When we reached this place—Yooldil Gabbi it is called—there was much activity. The invaders were there and had a built a new kind of pathway. It carved its way through the desert, cutting across our usual route. It was so long that there was no way to walk around it. It was constructed of felled trees laid across a high mound of stones piled upon the ground. On the trees lay two thin lines made of some kind of shiny rock. I knew how to carve and shape wood so that it was long, thin and perfectly straight. How they had managed to do this with rock defied my knowledge. On this pathway there travelled an enormous beast, a devil serpent. It was huge and the colour of charcoal. A haze of ash rained down around it, covering everything in its wake. Its insides appeared to be on fire. It spewed black smoke and hissed white clouds of water. It was intolerably loud, deafening even. When I first laid eyes on it I was very much afraid. My brothers assured me that it was bound to the pathway and would not deviate. As long as we kept our distance it would not harm us. Not only was this beast a horror to behold, it also required sustenance, and lots of it. It fed on water. Its appetite was so great that it was draining the sacred soak. It did not happen immediately, but the day was fast approaching when it would quench its thirst for the last time. Then the soak would be empty. It would have sucked the bowels of the earth dry. My ancestors would not have believed this was possible. This beast would do it though. And once the water was completely sapped it could never again be replenished. Of course, it would take many seasons before this happened and we continued to pass through this area as it was an important route. As with so many other things we had no choice, and when the soak was gone we were forced to find other means to sustain ourselves. By this time so much had changed that it was of little consequence.

At this place there lived a woman. She was pale like the other invaders but she was different. She had contact with the spirit world. Even though she appeared physically as a woman it was unclear if she was entirely from this world. The elders respected her and she protected us to some degree. She had the same weapons the invaders had, two small fire sticks. She kept the other invaders away with them, particularly their lawmen. I was wary of her, though. Not all spirits are to be trusted. Although she was kind to us and did her best to shelter us from the other invaders, far too many people became dependent on her. I thought this was a bad thing. They came to her for food and water and even entrusted some secrets to her. They called her Kabbarli, which means grandmother. The invaders called her Mrs. Bates.

She was against us mixing with children resulting from a relationship with an invader. She believed that our people would not survive, and those of us tainted with the seed of the invader were not the same. My father and grandfather had spoken to me about the invaders' attitude before. That they were against children that carried their own blood. I asked myself why. Was it not to their benefit that we learn to live together? These children were a bridge between our worlds. They were the future. My father had told me how things were when the invaders first arrived. At that time they came with their own animals but still shared the land and respected our sacred grounds. There were many good men among them who believed that we could live in harmony. It is not that way anymore. Now they want it all for themselves. The land is not any single person's property. Why is this so difficult to understand? The land is for all of us. We must respect it. It provides for us. It owns us, we don't own it. If we care for it, it cares for us.

This girl was one of these children. Her father had been a man who had walked with camels and had deserted her mother. I didn't have a problem with this, though. She was one of us. We were all from the same mother, from the land, so what did it matter that her father was an invader? He was no longer around anyway, and her mother was a strong and noble person. She upheld the law. If I was to be joined with her I would have to care for her mother anyway. Her father was less important.

In the past, courting a woman and making arrangements with her family had required a long ceremonial procedure. Now we were forced to make somewhat more haste. I felt it important to take her away from this place as soon as possible. I planned to head back towards our homelands where there would be less chance of being disturbed by the invaders. There was much discussion among my tribesmen concerning her suitability for me. Eventually I was able to convince them that she was of great importance to me and that I wouldn't leave without her. They proceeded to make the necessary arrangements with her family. I was relieved to hear that my spears were of sufficient quality to appease them.

Thankfully, enough among them hadn't become totally reliant on the invaders for sustenance and could make use of my weapons. I had seen the terrible results of relying exclusively on the invaders offerings, particularly at this place. Some people had even taken to wearing the invaders' coverings. They had even begun to smell like them, and the odour was putrid. They resorted to begging from the invaders that rode on the great black beast. There was even talk that certain women had offered themselves up as payment in return for food or water. I was astonished at how quickly our people had resorted to this sort of bartering. There was no honour in this. It only served to convince me further of the importance of leaving as quickly as possible and taking this woman away with me.

We set up camp some distance away from the invaders' pathway. I didn't want the spirit woman around either, but the elders accepted her so I had little choice. In the evening we began the marriage ceremony. Even though I had been through it once before I had forgotten some of the things I was obliged to do. One part of the ceremony involved my wife's mother. By law she was entitled to hurl abuse at me and I was not permitted to respond. I was somewhat perturbed that she protested about my inability to provide for her and her daughter. Had she not seen my spears? In any case, I put up with her rantings for as long as was necessary. It was just the way. This arrangement did have its advantages, though. After absorbing the sting of her words we were never allowed to communicate directly with each other again. That would have to be done through her daughter. It would also be my responsibility to ensure that she and her daughter were well cared for.

Once the ceremony was over I decided to leave as soon as possible. I will set out to follow the example of my grandfather. I will endeavour to go forward and educate my children correctly. Perhaps in time things will change and the land will be returned to our care. I do fear for the damage that will be done before this occurs. I have seen it in this place and all the other places where we can no longer go. I will do what is in my power. I will try and avoid contact with the invaders as best I can. The only place that is still safe is our homelands, as long as we avoid their spirit men. I hope it will stay that way and not be taken over like the other places. It is a place I know well. Everything is familiar to me there. The way the seasons change, all six of them. The land speaks to me there. It doesn't whisper. It cries in a loud voice. I call back to it and it answers me. I don't know how long we will have but I will persist until the day comes when we must find another sanctuary or things improve. I have even heard that they have proposed a special area for us. A state, they call it. A state of what? I can't see how that would work. The land is for all of us and should not be divided. It is a sorry situation, but somehow I don't feel that all hope is lost. I have found a new partner and we will face the future together.

FOUR

....

A CHANGE OF PLANS

MENS BUSINESS

Billy woke for the third time in as many days in a strange bed. He was relieved that at least one thing was consistent in all this. It was reassuring that it was still the same bed as the night before. He was beginning to feel like a nomad. It felt good. No responsibilities, no ties; just taking everything as it came; always on the move, goalless, yet not completely without direction. He began to think that he could get used to living this way. He didn't want to give up his obligations and responsibilities altogether, but having the freedom to decide when to act upon them was certainly more relaxing. He was surprised how quickly he was adapting to this new, laid-back approach.

He felt content in this new bed and with the feeling of comfort it offered. It was soft and luxurious, and he felt incredibly secure ensconced in it and its covers. He didn't feel like getting up; it was far too safe and warm. He was of the mindset that if anything were to break through the bedroom door then he would just pull the covers up over his head and ignore it. He lay there with his head enveloped by the pillow and stared up at the ceiling. Splattered across it were what appeared to be countless streaks and spots of dried blood. Scattered between the splatters were the remnants of a number of insects, mainly mosquitoes. He squinted and imagined it was a star map. A picture of some far-off constellation. He stopped squinting. It was beginning to make his forehead throb. On further inspection it looked as if someone had fought a private battle with a swarm of insect invaders. Judging by the amount of blood it was clear that the victim had not escaped entirely unscathed. It was also apparent that the bugs had not faired at all well and had suffered enormous losses.

Very gradually, and with some regret, he forced himself to get up and take in his new surroundings. With some effort he flung back the covers and swung his legs out of bed. His head thumped harder, reminding him of the events of the previous evening. He sat for a moment on the edge of the bed with his elbows resting on his knees and his head in his hands. He gingerly ran his fingers over the contours of the bandages covering his forehead. He hoped that one morning, in the not-too-distant future, he would wake up and not have to deal with a headache, be it self-inflicted or not. He scanned the room for his clothes and saw them neatly folded on a chair in the corner. A strong smell permeated the room. Somewhere in the house something was frying. It smelt good and his stomach growled in anticipation of nourishment. He stood up and padded across the room in his socks. On the way he passed the dresser. He stopped and laid his hands on top of it. He waited, thinking that there may be a surge of some kind of spiritual energy. There was nothing. Whatever had sat there the night before had left no trace. He searched the dresser and floor for a clue. No feathers today. Nevertheless, he remained convinced that what he had seen the night before was real. Physical evidence was no longer necessary.

He pulled on his clothes and noted dried blood down the front of his shirt. One of his first goals should be finding a washing machine. His attire was showing distinct signs of overuse, and Billy toyed with the idea of ditching them altogether. Starting with a new set of clothes might be a better option. He quickly pushed the thought aside. One obligation he certainly had to deal with was to find a phone and call his girlfriend. Once he had dealt with that he could move on to more mundane things, like cleanliness and personal hygiene. He took one last look at the bed and bid it a silent and regretful farewell. It had been warm and comforting, not unlike the womb, he mused.

He stealthily cracked open the bedroom door and stuck his head out. A long corridor ran past his room, with a series of doors on either side. In one direction it led to and terminated at the front door of the house. In the other lay an aromatic pathway. The smell of freshly fried food. His nostrils twitched. The choice was simple and for once he didn't need a moment to deliberate. He marched resolutely towards the smell. A small step at the end of the corridor led directly into a kitchen. Billy missed the step and set one foot down awkwardly, twisting his ankle and sending him stumbling into the room. He caught his balance on the kitchen table, causing it to slide across the floor, its legs screeching along the tiles. Doug, who was standing at the sink, whirled around in alarm.

'Whoa, watchit.'

'Sorry.'

'It's ok. Would have warned you about the step if I'd heard you coming.' He paused, taking Billy in. 'Fancy a bit o' tucker?'

Billy nodded enthusiastically.

'Take a seat then.'

Billy pulled out a metal-framed chair with no rubber feet. It also screeched across the floor, sending a shiver up his spine. Doug shot him another irritated glance but decided against reprimanding him again.

'Did you have a good sleep?'

'Yeah, great thanks. Head's a bit worse for wear, though.'

'I'm sure it'll heal. You might be feeling it for a few days, though. Took the trouble of patching it up for you last night.'

'I noticed.' Billy reached self consciously up to his forehead. 'Thanks.'

'No worries.'

Doug turned to the stove, scooped two eggs out of a spitting frypan and slid them onto a chipped enamel plate. Without moving his feet, he leant over to the table and unceremoniously skidded the plate across to Billy.

'You not having any?'

'Nah, already eaten.'

Billy spied a clock hanging above the stove and saw to his surprise that it was three-thirty.

'Wow! It's late.'

'You're right about that. Thought I'd let you sleep it off, though. I was hoping the smell of eggs'd wake you up.'

Billy beamed. 'Well, it worked.'

They sat in silence while Billy ate. It was his first decent meal in quite some time and he ravenously wolfed down the eggs. Doug studied him. He wondered if he should probe Doug about the significance of Pidgin, but as the food charged his body any lingering thoughts about the night before melted away. When he had finished, he leaned back in his chair with a satisfied grin.

'Hit the spot?'

'You bet,' said Billy. 'You don't live at the community?'

'No, too busy here. I do head out there once a week, though. I'm working on a dictionary of our language.'

'Oh?'

'For a long time I was pretty messed up. Alcohol was the big problem. Kind of took over my life and I totally forgot where I came from. I even forgot the traditional ways I'd been taught as a child. Thankfully, now that I've stopped wetting my brain, those memories are slowly coming back. The community helped me get off it. It's a dry zone, you know. Once I came out of the haze and felt strong enough

I moved back here. I've gotta tell you, though, one drop and I'd be back into that stuff. That's why I decided to keep myself busy and do something useful. Keeps me clean.'

'And that's the dictionary?'

'Well, yeah, that's one of the things I do. I think it's important to preserve some things while we still can. We need to educate our people so we can fend for ourselves. That's my big hope, anyway. As long as one of us keeps it alive, the culture will survive. The English used to think we were a dying race. Maybe some things are no more, but we're far from dead. We're still here. Some of the languages are also no more, but a lot still survive. I felt it was important to keep ours going. That's why I'm helping make a dictionary. Today our language group is becoming one of the strongest because of this. It wasn't until I started to educate myself that I really began to learn things.'

He started chuckling to himself.

'At school they taught me about Captain Cook and the *Endeavour* and other ships coming over the water. It didn't make any sense to me. I grew up in the middle of the desert and they were teaching me about ships and the sea. Things I'd never seen. How was I supposed to relate to that? I hadn't even seen the sea then, let alone a ship. What use are those things here? I was at school for five years and now really regret it. It's time I lost when I should've been learning the traditional ways. Education and bureaucracy are destroying everything. European education is breaking down our cultural identity. Bureaucracy is limiting everything we do. Now at least I can choose what I want to learn. I can educate myself the right way. I have found out so many things. We've had so many heroes. People that fought for equal pay for us in the Pilbara in the nineteen forties. Tjandamurra, who waged a guerrilla war against police in the Kimberleys. There are so many stories. They give me the strength to do what I am doing.'

As Doug spoke Billy's mind began to wander. It dawned on him how very little he knew about his own ancestry. It was a side of Australia he had never experienced. He had grown up near the coast and in urban surroundings. The man across the table had grown up in a completely different environment.

Doug sensed that he was losing his audience and cut his story short.

'But that's enough about me. What's your story? Where are your people from?'

'People?'

'Yeah, your language group, your tribe. You're a Nunga aren't you?'

'Huh?' Billy was perplexed. There was that word again. Rob had used it as well: people.

'You've got Aboriginal ancestry don't you? That fella wouldn't have shown up last night if you were white.'

'Who?'

'Um, the fella in your room.'

'Pidgin?'

'He didn't tell me his name, but yeah, that's who I mean.'

'My mum was Aboriginal. Don't know much about her, though. She died when I was really young.'

'Sorry to hear that.'

'It's ok. My dad took good care of me.'

They sat for a moment in silence. Billy's demeanour changed as he thought about his parents. 'He's gone too.'

'Your dad?'

'Yeah, they both got cancer.'

Again there was silence. Billy stared at his empty plate and studied the remnants of egg yolk drying on it.

Doug changed the subject. 'What brings you up this way?'

Billy sighed and looked up from his plate. 'Series of coincidences, I guess. To be perfectly honest, I'm not really sure how I got here. I should be getting back home, though. I'm supposed to get married.'

Doug leant into the table and sucked air in quickly through his teeth. Billy noted that he was missing one of his front teeth and wondered if it was a battle scar from his drinking days. 'Married?'

'Yeah. If I've got the days right, I think I may have left someone standing at the altar.'

Doug leaned back again in his chair and exhaled through pursed lips. 'That's not good.'

'No, not at all; but I'm sort of having doubts about the whole thing, to tell the truth.'

'Well, you can't just not do nothin'. Maybe you'd better give her a call?'

'That was the plan. I suppose I've gotta face the music sometime. Just not sure what the hell I'm gonna say.'

Doug studied Billy's face. 'I suggest you tell her the truth. If she really cares about you she'll give you the time to think. Too many people get married these days without thinking it through, and then it doesn't last. You gotta be sure 'bout what you're doing. I should know. I've messed up enough in the past.'

Billy was buoyed by Doug's words. He stared down at his empty plate again for a moment before looking up at Doug. 'Do you think I could use your phone?'

Doug shook his head. 'Really like to help you there, but it's been disconnected. Normally pretty good with those things but just plain forgot to pay the bill. There's a phone box around the corner, though. I used it yesterday, so it should be working as long as no one's trashed it again.'

'Ok, then I'll go make the call.'

Doug's face was brightened by a broad grin. 'Good, better get it over and done with, eh?'

Billy returned an insecure smile. 'Yep.'

He made a move to slide back his chair but the look on Doug's face reminded him not to inflict more scraping on the tiles. He twisted sideways in the chair and stood up using the table as leverage.

'I'll see you soon.'

'You can use the back door,' said Doug, indicating behind him with a flick of his thumb. 'The front one's a bit jammed so you better come back the same way.'

Billy's body hung in mid stride for a moment. He nodded to Doug, took a deep breath and managed to coax himself into forward motion. Doug gave him a big smile of encouragement, and then

Billy flung open the screen door and stepped outside.

BREAKING THE ENGAGEMENT

Beth was ropable. She screamed down the receiver. 'How the hell could you do this to me?'

Having finally summoned up the courage to ring his fiancée, Billy was now already regretting the decision. He knew beforehand that he was going to get a drubbing but still wasn't entirely prepared for her ferocious reaction. At first she had been genuinely concerned about him but her frustration had got the better of her. She had called his friends and nobody had known his whereabouts. They had tried to reassure her that he would turn up. It was now clear that this was not going to happen.

'Beth, I ...'

'I'm guessing you thought it was quite ok just to up sticks and leave me sitting here with all the arrangements. Do you have any idea how many people are crying for your blood here? Good thing we were doing this in my parents' backyard and not in a church. We managed to postpone everything, but it's costing them a fortune. I hope you're satisfied.'

As she spoke her voice gradually rose further in pitch and volume. Billy moved the handset away from his ear to reduce the onslaught. It felt heavy in his hand. It was a solid piece of plastic and would have made a good weapon if it wasn't securely attached to the box.

He was in a metal-framed, glass telephone box around the corner from Doug's house. Thankfully it hadn't taken very long to find it. After the cool interior of Doug's house, it had been a shock to step out into a very hot day. The sun had beat down heavily on him as he made his way down the street. Upon spotting the box, he had rushed to it and jumped in, expecting it to provide welcome shelter from the onslaught from above.

The telephone box itself had seen better days. One pane of safety glass was shattered but had remained in place. It was split into thousands of small, neat squares and was no longer transparent but opaque and milky white. It had evidently received a substantially hard knock, possibly from another duped lover. The interior of the booth was coated in graffiti, including the phone itself, and it stank. It had apparently been used recently as a urinal. Billy equated the phone box to his present state: slightly battered and somewhat worse for wear. He couldn't ascertain which of them smelt better. His need for a shower was dire. He looked around self-consciously, peering through the glass and hoping nobody outside could hear her yelling. Her voice filled the box and was further amplified as it reverberated off the glass walls. Through the gaps in the graffiti he scanned the street outside. It was deserted. The interior of the box didn't offer as much shelter from the sun as he had envisaged. It was incredibly hot and he thought he would pass out any minute. It was an oversized, glass-sided oven. He tried propping the door open with his foot to let in some air, but only succeeded in getting his sneaker wedged in the gap between the door and its frame. All he wanted to do was to get out of the box as quickly as possible.

He gave up the fight to escape for a moment and reflected on why he was in the box. He had strong feelings for Beth but realised that the attraction didn't run as deeply as he had thought. Before finding himself in his present predicament, he hadn't seriously considered what it would mean to spend the rest of his life with her. He could understand her irritation, but now he felt his eyes had been opened. A new world had presented itself to him. After his experiences with Pidgin and the talk with Doug he realised there were important things about himself and his identity that he had to investigate. He had to find out more. Beth couldn't help him with this, and he doubted she would even be interested in such a thing. They were going in different directions. Her goal and main preoccupation in life was to get hooked. She thought she would be over the hill and unmarriageable if she couldn't find a spouse by the age of twenty-five. He didn't want the life she had envisaged for them. Deep down he felt a responsibility to do more than just be a husband and a breadwinner. He let her words flow over him. They were no longer of any real importance. He did feel guilty and knew it wasn't entirely fair on her. It wasn't all her fault. She wasn't the problem, he was.

'So, what's her name?'

'Pardon?'

'The girl, the one that seems more important to you than me.'

'There isn't anyone else.'

'You expect me to believe that? There must be a reason why you took off. I can kind of understand that you probably needed a last fling before you settled down.'

Billy was confused. What was her game? It surprised him. She really didn't know him. He may be many things, but if he committed himself to someone he remained true to them. He wouldn't be able to bring himself to be with another. If there was one thing his father had taught him, it was a moral responsibility to your partner. He decided to try a different tactic and explain his predicament.

'It's nothing like that, Beth. I've just found myself in a strange situation and I'm trying to deal with it. I need some time to myself. Time to think.'

'Time? What do you mean time? Haven't you had enough of that already?'

Trying to dress it all up wouldn't work. She just wasn't capable of understanding what he was going through. 'Ok, to be perfectly honest, at the moment I don't see this whole marriage thing working for me.'

There, he'd said it. This was something new for him. He wasn't usually so outspoken about his feelings and had no idea what the reaction would be. He braced himself for another barrage of words. To his surprise there was silence at the other end of the line. He waited. The sweat on his forehead had built up and a drop ran down over his eyebrow and into his eye. The salty water stung and he squinted hard before wiping his face with the back of his sleeve. The squinting irritated the large bump on his forehead and his head started pounding again. He was finding it difficult to concentrate and began feeling faint from the heat in the box.

When Beth eventually replied she was surprisingly composed but still spat out her words venomously. 'You call me reverse-charges and then break up with me. Who the fuck do you think you are?'

He heard ruffling and clattering in the earpiece and then an abrupt and conclusive click, followed by the dial tone. Billy stared at the telephone receiver before slowly holstering it in its cradle. Absentmindedly he pushed the change button and felt inside the change hole for coins. To his surprise there was a twenty-cent piece in it. He flipped the coin slowly over in the palm of his hand with his thumb. He stared nonplussed at it for a minute, feeling completely spent and empty. He began to contemplate what he had just done. Suddenly his legs went to jelly and he felt nauseous. Not only was he overcome by the heat in the box but also by the gravity of the situation. He desperately fought with the door, but his sneaker remained caught in it. He braced himself against the wall and used his other leg to push against the door. His foot miraculously released itself from his sneaker which was launched onto the street as the door flew open. He fell forward and stumbled outside before sinking to his knees and panting. There was a slight breeze. After the stifling environment of the glass box, it felt light and refreshing on his face, almost as if he was kneeling in front of an open refrigerator door. He sucked in the cooling air, closed his eyes and tilted his head to the sky. He spent a moment absorbing everything that had just happened. He felt a weight lift from his shoulders. He breathed out heavily, unintentionally blowing a raspberry in the process. He sat back on his ankles, opened his eyes and focussed on calming himself. He waited until his breathing had returned to normal. He then dragged himself to his feet and dusted off the knees of his jeans. He retrieved his sneaker, wiped some loose dirt off his sock and pulled it on.

He took a quick look around to get his bearings before striding back towards Doug's house with as much haste as he could muster. Even though he felt mentally drained, new energy coursed through his body. With every step he felt some of his previous worries fall behind him. By the time he had rounded the corner into Doug's street he felt like a new man, liberated from his responsibilities and released to continue on into whatever lay ahead.

AN INVITATION

Billy had just fought an extensive battle with Doug's front door. He had tugged and pulled at it and become increasingly frustrated. After he had wrestled unsuccessfully with it for a time, and eventually exhausted himself, he remembered that Doug had told him not to bother even trying. The gravity of his conversation with Beth had flooded back and overcome him, diverting his attention. It had taken a fruitless struggle with the door before he could settle himself. The whole gamut of emotions had run through him, from rage to sorrow to despair. The door had become a useful foil on which to vent all of this. He took a step back and eyed it for a moment. He then let out a long sigh, straightened himself up and set off around the side of the house.

He rounded the rear corner of the house and into the backyard to see Doug, Rob and Tex sitting in a tight semi-circle under a wilting fruit tree. Doug was holding court and telling the other men a story. Upon seeing Billy he invited him to sit down. Rob stood with a concerned look on his face.

'Are you ok?'

'Yeah, I'll live.'

Rob told him that he had heard about what happened the night before. 'That fella is trouble. You want us to get him for you? You don't deserve to be treated that way.'

Billy was taken aback. He hadn't even considered retribution. Not only that, he had completely forgotten the previous evening's events. He had initially assumed Rob was talking about his girlfriend. In any case, violence was the last thing on his mind. 'No thanks. It's not necessary.'

Rob shrugged. 'Up to you I guess.'

He turned his attention to Doug, and Billy willingly followed his lead. He wasn't yet in a state to discuss anything of consequence.

'I was just telling the boys about how things were when I was growing up in the desert. Everything was about water. In the desert you don't talk a lot. It's a matter of survival. Talking drains you of moisture and scares off prey. When I was young we were taught to suck on stones to keep our mouths wet.' He paused and chuckled to himself. 'Of course, for my parents it had the added advantage of shutting me up.'

Doug stopped smiling and a stern look flashed across his face. 'As a child I was expected to listen well to them. If I didn't it could've cost me my life. Maybe I should give you fellas a stone to suck on once in a while.'

The two young men squirmed uncomfortably in their chairs.

'Like I said, water was pretty hard to come by then. You wouldn't think it looking around today.'

On his trip to and from the telephone box Billy had seen an enormous amount of standing water.

'You're not kidding, uncle,' said Rob. 'I heard they even cancelled the Henley-on-Todd today, those silly buggers can't run their race, because for a change, there's water in the river!'

Doug silenced him with a look and continued.

'Paying attention and staying quiet were really important. Now you guys have guns so it makes it easier to hunt. Back then we only had spears. I've got a bit rusty at it but I'm still pretty good at throwing them.' He turned to Rob and Tex. 'Gonna have to take you fellas out and do it the old way one of these days.'

Rob and Tex nodded.

'When we was hunting kangaroo you'd have to be completely silent. We used to do it in pairs and only use sign language to communicate. Kangaroos are pretty wary buggers so it would be a case of trying to get as close as possible without them noticing. If you watch their ears you can tell if they've noticed you or not. It's pretty hard work and you have to be really accurate with your throwing. You only get one shot. You've gotta keep real still. You know, make like a tree. Takes a lot of practice. Reckon you fellas would have a bit of trouble doing it. You can't sit still now.'

The three young men looked at each other and shuffled in their seats.

'See what I mean? Always fidgeting.'

He leant back in his chair and smirked at them with his arms folded. The chair, a rusty garden stool, creaked under his weight. Billy thought it would collapse at any moment. Doug was a man of very generous proportions.

Doug looked over his shoulder and indicated the setting sun. 'This was the most dangerous time of day. Your enemy could come out of the sunlight and you wouldn't see him coming. As a kid my parents would tell me stories, to scare me I guess, but it worked. It kept me close to them and I didn't wander off. One of the stories was about a caveman. You wanna hear it?'

The men nodded as one.

'This story comes from a place thirty k's south of here where the caveman is now represented by a rock. The rock appears to leave the cave as you approach the site. This story was told to children, to put 'em off leaving the camp alone.'

Doug took a deep breath, leant towards his audience and lowered his voice. 'The caveman lived in a cave by a waterhole. He had children, little devil children, who lived with him in the cave. They all lived off human flesh. The caveman would wait for a weary traveller to come down to his waterhole. He would then invite the traveller to stay, offering him his fire and a windbreak. The traveller would settle by the fire, relenting to the caveman's pleas of loneliness and need for company. The caveman'd then begin to sing a song in his own language. The words of the song when translated were the worst kind of swear words and abuse. All of this was directed at the unsuspecting traveller. After a while the traveller would slip into a deep sleep, listening to the caveman's monotonous song. The caveman would check every now and then to see if his guest was still awake.'

Doug leant back in his stool and it groaned in protest. With his upper body he began to articulate the caveman's movements.

'When he was sure he was asleep he'd spring to his feet with his song getting louder and faster. He'd then run to the cave and return with his waddie. He'd strike his slumbering guest across the bridge of the nose, killing him.'

Doug swung an imaginary club in front of the faces of the men and instinctively they pulled their heads back to avoid it.

'He would then dismember the body and feed it to his crying devil children. This went on for a long time and the people camped in the area couldn't work out why so many of their people were disappearing. A man was selected to go and investigate the problem. One day he came across the caveman's camp. The man was invited to stay. He was also sung to sleep. However, the man was smart, and only pretended to sleep. The caveman, believing that the man slept, sprang to his feet and went to the cave for his waddie. The man placed a log where he had been lying, took his spears and hid behind the windbreak. The caveman returned from the cave and with all his might he struck the log.'

Doug practically yelled the last half of the sentence, startling his audience.

'Realising his mistake too late the caveman stood up. The man threw his spear, injuring the caveman. He then finished him off and burnt his body. The man then took fire with him and went into the cave. The little devil children were inside, crying for the best parts of the body: the eyes, the lips, the sexual organs. Enraged, the man killed the children and then set fire to the cave. He then returned to his camp and told his people that the danger was over.'

Doug stopped to catch his breath and scanned the faces of the three men. They sat in silence, waiting for him to speak.

'It's an old story, but when I was young it did its job. I always stayed close to our camp. But even old stories are important. They might change over time, though. You see, there are no hard and fast rules. Everything keeps moving. Nature doesn't stand still, and nor do we. We have to adapt. We don't have a Bible, we have guidelines. If an elder dies and doesn't feel that there is someone responsible to take on his stories, he will take them with him to the grave. Every rock, every tree has significance. Over time what they represent might also change. If old stories are lost, someone who feels responsible will take what they know. They'll write a new story. That cave is still dangerous. There's lots of rock slides there, especially with rain like we've just had. So the story still has a purpose.'

Doug turned his focus to Billy.

'Now, we are kinda lucky. We no longer have to live off the land exclusively. We have modern things to make life easier. That doesn't mean we should ignore what we already know. In my own lifetime I have gone from living off the land to living in this house. My bed used to be on the ground between my brothers and sisters next to a campfire.'

He waved his hands over the ground in front him and rubbed them together as if warming them over a fire.

'We used to sleep with our parents next to the fire and older kids on the outside. Us younger kids would sleep in the middle to keep us warm and safe, and prevent us from rolling into the fire. The older kids were warned that the spiritual man would come and get them if they slept next to the fire. Maybe I'll tell you about him later. Now I sleep in sheets and out of the elements. It's been a radical change but I don't forget where I came from. I like it out there. If I don't regularly spend time in the bush I feel lost. Like I have no mother. I pine for it. Having said that, I don't want to go back to living fulltime out there. This is much better. I've found a middle ground. There always needs to be some kind of balance.'

Billy shifted in his chair, feeling a bit uncomfortable that he was now the centre of attention.

'Only recently a tribe came out of the bush. They were oblivious to everything that had happened in this country. They hadn't seen a car before or white men. They were shocked and scared when they were confronted with those things. They was even prepared to put up a fight to defend themselves. It took quite a bit to persuade 'em to go with those white fellas. They only went with them when they recognised one of their own tribesmen that they'd been separated from years before. Some of them stayed in this new society but some of them couldn't cope. They went back out into the desert. I'm sure they weren't the last. It's a big country. Either way, everyone has to find his or her own balance.'

Billy stared off blankly into the distance. His mind had begun to wander and thoughts of his own search for balance were troubling him.

'How'd it go with your girl?'

Billy turned his attention to the dirt on the ground between his feet. He studied it pensively for a moment and then raised his head and looked up at Doug. 'She's not my girl anymore. It's over.'

There they were, the two words he had never thought he'd be using. He had been struggling on and off with his marital predicament since the moment he had woken up on the bus. The words seemed so final. However, in their finality they brought relief. He had faced up to something which he had known wasn't right in the first place. He had tackled the situation head on. It had taken him a while to get it done. Making tough choices always seemed to take him a lot of time. Now that it was done, he felt as if an enormous weight had been lifted. He realised Doug had been in some way responsible for helping him to make the decision.

'Thanks for giving me a bit of a push.'

'It was nothing,' said Doug.

Billy felt concerned that he was outstaying his welcome but was at loss about what to do next. He breathed deeply and looked out timidly at Doug from under his eyebrows. 'Do you think it would be ok if I stayed here for a while?'

Doug shifted in his stool and looked Billy squarely in the eye. 'Well, I've been hav'n a bit of a think about your situation. So I had a chat before with the boys,' said Doug, flicking a thumb towards Rob and Tex. 'I think it might be better if you go back out to the community with them for a while. You won't have much, just a roof over your head, but it'll give you some time to work out what you wanna do next. They can always use an extra set of hands out there. Who knows, maybe you'll learn something. What was it you said you did back in the city?'

'I just finished studying to be an accountant.'

There was a moment of silence and then all three men burst into laughter. Rob nearly fell off his stool before managing to compose himself. 'Hope you're up ta gettin your hands dirty then.'

Billy ignored their response, still slightly taken aback by their generosity. 'Are you sure it's ok?'

Rob and Tex stopped smirking and chimed in unison. 'Yeah, no worries.'

'Then it's settled,' said Doug.

Rob took the comment as an indication that they should leave. He stood, interlocked his fingers and stretched his arms above his head. His back cracked under the strain. 'Ok, let's get a move on then.'

WELL 15, MANJANKA

....

1906

We thought the dry times were over and the land could provide for us again. But the rain has brought with it a new threat. The invaders have come to take our water. They have encroached further into our homelands and have already taken over some of our most reliable waterholes. They have brought with them an enormous number of their own animals. These creatures require great quantities of water and are draining our sources. We still have the soaks but they are under threat as well. They have dug some of them out to get down to the water deep in the bowels of the earth and have built something they call a well around them. Because of this we can no longer readily access the soaks. We have already lost one of our warriors when he fell into one of these holes trying to access the water. He drowned before we could get to him. We would never dig a deep hole, only a shallow one and then, using a hollow reed, we would stick it into the ground and drink our fill. As with all things we only take whatever we need and leave it intact for others to use. There is a fine balance with these water sources and it is far better to let the land run its course than to change it. Without water we are surely doomed.

Over the course of the preceding seasons there was no rain whatsoever. The sky had turned to bone. We had prepared for this eventuality as we always do. It transpires from time to time that the land cannot provide sufficiently for us. Through careful planning we have always found a way to get through difficult periods. We see the signs leading up to this and make ourselves ready for it. We amass food and keep it in storage, but we are still required to tighten our hair strings in order to ensure that our meagre supplies will last. It is not always clear when the dry will come to an end. The spiritual men can give advice but they are also bound by the information that the land supplies. These past seasons of dry were particularly long and harsh. At one stage, and as a last resort, we had even considered going to the invaders for help. Our supplies were severely depleted. This would have meant doing things against our will. We were not prepared to do this and my fathers decided not to have anything to do with them at all. At least not directly. On a number of occasions we did manage to kill one or two of their animals. The risks were great, though, and we were in continual fear of reprisals. Our defences are weak as our warriors no longer have the numbers to fight them effectively. Many seasons ago they stormed our camp and we lost a great many of our womenfolk. Thankfully, we were able to marry into neighbouring tribes and in doing so could keep the family going. It has been a great relief to successfully build our numbers again.

It is a further consolation that the spiritual men have been successful and the dry has come to an end. The sky has opened and water is flowing once again. However, with the returning rains, the invaders have taken the opportunity to ensconce themselves further into our territory. We now find ourselves in a dire predicament. We no longer face solely a struggle with the land. Another dilemma is afflicting us and it has taken on a human form.

At present I am being held captive along with several other men from our family. They have bound us together by the neck so that we cannot run away. We are tied to one of their animals and are being dragged along behind it. Linked like this, we are like a snake made out of men. One of us has already been killed and we fear that more of us will succumb before they have obtained what they seek. They want to know where the water sources are. Once found, they will destroy the soak and dig one of their own holes. This will make it impossible for us to access it in the future. The bindings hurt. They cut into my shoulders and the material, a kind of stone, becomes extremely hot in the sun. It burns into my neck. We do not have the tools to remove them and no longer have weapons to defend ourselves. They have been taken away. All they are feeding us is a kind of meat which is treated in some way and dries our throats. The thirst is terrible. It will not be long before we are forced to succumb and reveal where the water is. If only to ensure our survival.

Before this happened we had been returning to the sacred rockhole. It is the only place where there is always water. In the dry it is our last refuge. The area has always been protected for times such as those we have just experienced. It is there that we put our food in storage. There is also shade. We do not disturb the trees in the area nor cut the wood for our fires. We hollow out shallow holes beneath the trees and wait out the heat of the day there. The rockhole is our lifeline in difficult times and when there is no other source of sustenance. It is not only a sanctuary for us but also for our animal totems. There they wait at the waters, just as we do, for the rains to return. Once they come, as they just have, we then spread out again like the budgerigar across the land. Until then we conserve our energy. The sacred waters must be protected at all costs for man and beast alike.

Now that they have taken us with them we are obliged to find water for them, but we dare not lead them to these sacred waters. Our only hope is that they will be satisfied with what we give them and then leave us in peace. I fear this will not be the case. The invaders never seem to be completely satisfied. I am not alone with this feeling. We all fear that once they have what they want they will kill us all. If only to conceal what they have done. We are like vermin to them. We are only useful for specific things and then thrown away afterwards. In our culture we have a mutual understanding. We don't own anything; it is for all of us. What we have we share. The land gives us these things. It is a valuable gift. It is not for us to say who should possess them. What is now being done is an extremely dishonourable thing. Even the invaders must understand this. Yet they are driven by something else. A desire to be the sole owner of something. They are blinded by these desires. It takes them over and they can only see what they can gain for themselves. They take and give nothing in return. We would never do that. If we were to live this way we would not survive. We understand the lore: that without fair trade and interaction, all of us will suffer. Not just our own people but everyone, the invaders included. Right now we can do very little to change their attitude. They are bent only on attaining the goal they see directly before their eyes. They don't understand that what they do in the short term will have devastating effects in the time to come. They don't see the repercussions of their actions. If they take the water and make it unavailable to all then the water itself will eventually stop flowing. Then we will all have to go without.

Above all I am shocked and distressed at how quickly this is happening. The changes have been too substantial and too rapid. It is beyond comprehension. We are very adaptable. The land has taught us this. Yet this goes far beyond the land alone. I have a responsibility to care for my family. I need to protect my wife and children. I cannot do that from where I am now. My wife is with child at this very moment. I fear for them as I fear for myself. As a child I saw what the invaders are truly capable of. I remember well the day they swept through our camp and slaughtered my mothers, sisters and brothers. All our men lost someone that day. Thankfully I survived that ordeal by hiding myself. My own sons are not yet men. I must return to them and finish their training. They still have some way to go. They will need my knowledge to survive. My family is the one thing above all others that drives me to find a way out of this situation. I am certain I can escape the invaders once again. After all, I have done it before. There are no guarantees, though. We have been secretly communicating in sign language and have begun to formulate a plan. Only the bindings stand in our way. We are staying alert and hoping that an opportunity will arise. I will not let these pale demons send me to the spirit world. It is not a good day to die.

FIVE

....

BACK TO THE COMMUNITY

DORIS

Billy had just stepped out of the shower. He had never felt so clean in his entire life. His last shower had been just before going to his buck's party and this was his first serious attempt at cleanliness since then. It had been a huge relief to peel off his clothes and get totally naked. He hadn't thought that just standing under a steady flow of water could be so uplifting. In the backyard Doug had told him how traditionally they had never washed with water. It was much too precious. They had used smoke. Billy decided that there were some things he could do without but a refreshing shower wasn't one of them. When he eventually finished showering he felt like a new man and was firm in the opinion that smoke just couldn't equate to water. The supply of hot water hadn't lasted very long, though, before it had plummeted in temperature.

This hadn't deterred him and he had let the cold water flow over him until shivering had set in. He had stepped out only when the clattering of his teeth had begun to strain his jaw.

He stood dripping on the tiled floor with his eyes closed and waited until the heat of his surroundings began to elevate his body temperature. Eventually he stopped shaking. Only then did he open his eyes. Looking down at his naked body he decided his first task should be to search for a new set of underwear. Rob had lent him some clothing but underwear was one item which Billy considered should remain exclusive to the individual who wore it. He didn't feel it was the sort of thing you shared. Pangs of hunger suddenly pierced his stomach. Food, as usual, was his first concern. He relegated the search for fresh underwear to a minor priority and decided to go without it for the time being. He added it to the mental list of problems he still had to solve. He dressed himself and set about scraping something together to eat. From previous experience he knew the cabin had nothing to offer. He made up his mind to see if he could find something appetising at the general store.

Upon stepping out of the cabin Billy was enveloped by a cacophony of noise. It was early morning and thousands of birds were heralding the day. The bush had come alive. Billy marvelled at the sound. On exiting the cabin on his first morning, everything had seemed so dry and lifeless. It was as if without the scorching, midday rays of the sun everything had come out of hiding and felt free to express itself. The noise represented life itself. It was certainly thriving here. He stopped and listened, letting the warbling and chattering flow over him. It was invigorating. It gave him energy.

The ground beneath his sneakers was still cold from the night before and a chill rose up his legs. A crisp breeze played over his skin, making the hairs on his arms stand up. He stepped forward into a corridor of sunshine which was cutting its way between the cabins. He turned his face towards the light source. Its brightness made him squint but it failed to provide much warmth. It had yet to make its impression on the day. He rubbed and shook his arms. He jumped up and down on the spot. His blood began to circulate but he wasn't rewarded with an elevation in body temperature. He blew warm air into the palms of his hands, checked his bearings and moved off towards the shop.

Billy strode immediately to the rear of the store and stood in front of the freezers, whereupon he lost his momentum. He stared at the glass doors and was once again racked by thoughts of his predicament. He wasn't entirely sure why he had come back to the community or what he was going to do with his time there. He watched the icy water running in rivulets down the inside of the doors. At least the water had a purpose, he mused. It was going somewhere, even if it only ended up in a puddle gathering at the bottom of the freezer. Every droplet would find its way there eventually. Compared to him, the droplets had it all sorted out. They at least knew where they were going. He, on the other hand, felt no nearer his target. Whatever that was.

He stood deep in thought for a time, mulling over his situation and gazing glassy eyed at the freezers. After a moment he pushed the thoughts aside. He shook his head, trying to clear them from his consciousness. He didn't have any answers and it was pointless to get bogged down. He brought his eyes into focus and took a closer look at his reflection in the glass. The swelling on his face had subsided. Before stepping into the shower he had removed his bandages and hadn't bothered to replace them. He pressed his index finger gently around the wound on his forehead. It still hurt. At least now it looked better than it felt. He guessed it would take a few days before it completely cleared up. He was pretty sure he wouldn't have any permanent scarring.

'Did you find it?'

'Wuh?'

'Your way home.'

Billy spun around. Doris stood a few steps away with a smile upon her face.

'No. Not yet.'

Doris scrutinised his face.

'Looks like you've been in the wars.'

Billy dropped his hand self-consciously from his forehead.

'You might say that.'

'Yeah, you need to be bit careful with those fellas in Alice.'

'You heard what happened?'

'A little bit. Mabel told me. Don't really need to know the details, though. It's one reason we keep it dry around here. The grog has done a lot of damage in the past.'

Billy nodded solemnly.

So, have you decided what y' gonna do?'

'Ahem, no.'

'Maybe you should hook up with some of the boys. You already seem to be getting on pretty well with Rob. They can show you around and we can always use a bit of help around here. We've also got a bit of a cattle station which needs managing. Maybe you can help out with that.'

Billy was indeed getting to know Rob and realised he at least had a starting point. The idea of working a cattle farm was completely foreign to him, though, and he assumed he would require some basic stockman experience. He also cringed when he remembered their laughing at the announcement that he was an accountant and didn't think they would have much faith in his rural abilities.

'Don't know that I'll be much good doing that. Can't say that I've ever been on horse and I can't speak cow.'

'No worries. I'm sure you'll pick it up. You got this far, didn't you?'

Yes, thought Billy. He had made some progress. He was capable of adapting to something new. Doris's words buoyed his confidence. He took a deep breath and puffed out his chest.

'Yeah, you're right.'

Doris's face lit up watching Billy's posture change.

'Tell you what, if you ever just wanna chat, you come and see me. I'm in the house at the end of the street and my door is always open.'

Billy smiled in gratitude.

'Maybe you should just start by getting your bearings a bit. If you go behind the big hall out

back of the shop here, you'll find a path. If you follow it, it'll take you up the hill behind the town.
There's a great view from up there.'

'Thanks, I'll do that.'

'And once you're up there, you can follow the
path a bit further. It leads to a little waterhole. It's
kind of a sacred place for us. I don't have time today but maybe later in the week I can show you
around up there. One of the boys can do it too, of
course.'

'That would be great.'

'Good. Like I said, I've got some things to do.
Gonna have to be getting off. You have fun explor-
ing, ok?'

Billy felt the urge to shake her hand, or perhaps
even give her a hug. He was so grateful to have
some purpose again. He had to stop himself. He
barely knew the woman. He settled for a broad
smile and a nod. 'Thanks, I will.'

Doris walked down the aisle towards the cash
register. Billy quickly scoured the shop for some
basic supplies, eventually settling on some eggs and
bread. He would make himself a decent breakfast
and then follow Doris's advice and climb the hill.
He completely forgot about his underwear situation. After paying for his shopping he stepped out
into the street. Looking to his right and down to-

wards the end he saw a well-maintained house with a collection of flowering shrubs in front of it. Doris was climbing the stairs onto its verandah. She turned, saw him standing there and gave him a friendly wave. He overzealously returned the gesture and then felt self-conscious that he was being a little too enthusiastic. She acknowledged his wave and gestured up and towards his right. Billy turned back and looked where she was indicating. A hill rose steeply behind the shop. He looked back down the street to thank Doris but she had already gone into her house. He shrugged and with a renewed lightness in his stride made his way back to the cabin.

THE ROCKHOLE

Billy wandered up the hill behind the town. The dirt road narrowed until it became a small track, only wide enough for one person to traverse. The bush on either side closed in around him and blocked his view of the surrounding landscape. Slowly the track became steeper and he was climbing up, away from the desert floor. At some point the scrub thinned out and was gradually replaced with rock. Billy stopped for a moment to catch his breath. He was glad he had made himself a decent meal. The exertion of the climb was starting to sap his energy. He turned and looked behind him. He could now see the town in its entirety below him. It was incredibly small. A jumble of little white houses, their corrugated-iron roofs glinting in the sun. He could make out the main street, carving its way through the centre of the town before coming to an abrupt halt at a house to his right, on the edge of the town. Doris's dwelling. To his left it exited the town and stretched in a straight line away from him and far into the distance before being swallowed up by the bush. He now had a better overview of where he was. The town was nestled at the foot of a low mountain range and on the edge of a wide plain. In the distance he could see another line of hills running parallel to those he was presently on. It was as if the town lay in an enormous river bed. A wide, expansive river that stretched almost as far as the eye could see. Billy recalled reading that at one time the centre of Australia had been inundated by an inland sea. Looking at the vista before him he could clearly visualise the whole place under water. The hill he was climbing had perhaps once been a steep river bank. What existed now was another story. Even with the recent heavy rains everything still appeared brown and burnt. It all looked so incredibly dry and shimmered in the merciless heat. He looked down at his feet and was surprised to see wild flowers growing on the side of the track. Their vivid colours sprang out of their dry, brown surroundings. Clearly the rain had penetrated deep enough into the hard soil to provide nourishment for whatever lay beneath. It had revived this new vegetation from its dormant state.

He looked out across the plain once more. He squinted. On closer inspection he could make out splashes of colour emerging from the brown palate. The desert was coming to life. Maybe it wasn't as inhospitable as he had first assumed.

Billy continued up the hill. It was just before midday and the heat and the climb swiftly took their toll. The exertion depleted him of all his energy and he was relieved when the path dived into a narrow crevice, shaded by steep cliff faces on either side. He had set out entirely unprepared. He had no food or water, but going back straight away wasn't an option. First he would need to find a place to rest. He forged on further. The scrub gradually melted away, revealing only bare rock. The crevice slowly opened out and he found himself standing in a large, natural amphitheatre. It was sheltered on all sides by high, craggy rock faces. The ground beneath his feet was also solid rock and devoid of vegetation. It was polished smooth, with gentle undulations. Water lay in small pockets where the rock floor was more deeply eroded. Beneath a sheer cliff face in the far corner Billy could see a pond. It was bordered with low bushes. He stumbled over the uneven ground towards it. Upon reaching it he saw it was a lot larger than he had expected. The pond extended out to one side of the enclosed area through another break in the rocks. Although he could see no movement on its surface Billy assumed it was a natural catchment where the water had run down from the rocks around the corner. He was parched and covered in sweat. There was a large opening between the bushes and the rocky floor sloped down into the pond. He walked down the slope and knelt beside the pond. Leaning over the water he cupped his hands and dipped them into it. He splashed some of it into his face before throwing some down his dry throat. It was cool and refreshing.

All of a sudden an uncomfortable feeling swept over him and a cold shiver ran down his spine. He sensed that he was no longer alone. Billy raised his gaze and to his surprise saw Pidgin sitting on a small ledge protruding out of the rock face above the water. He stared directly at Billy and was almost within arm's reach. Billy sucked in his breath and scampered quickly backwards, away from the water's edge and onto the dusty surface of the rock floor. Billy looked up again at Pidgin and their eyes met. Billy felt drawn into them. He shifted position. Moving slightly forward towards Pidgin on his hands and knees, he stopped and sat back on his ankles. Their eyes remained locked. Billy focussed solely on Pidgin's pupils, which even in the daylight glowed strangely. Everything else in his field of vision blurred and melted away until Billy saw only those eyes. A voice in his head softly told him to close his eyes. Billy obeyed. His entire body went limp and his head slumped forward, his chin coming to rest upon his chest.

A myriad of images flickered rapidly through his mind. It was as if a camera was taking snapshots with a flash. Each time there was a spark of light an image sprang out at him. They began in rapid succession, flowing by as in a flip book. The images flashed by as if spat out by an old slide projector, before slowing and gradually coming to rest on a single image. Billy began to perceive movement within the stationary image, like a fragment of film. This was not only a visual experience; there were other sensory attributes. He could taste and smell and feel. The film played out for a short period, followed by another rapid burst of images. They slowed again, settled on a solitary image, and another little film followed. This sequence repeated itself.

In the first 'movie' that played out in Billy's head he saw a woman lying in a hospital bed. She was in excruciating pain. She writhed on the bed and bared her teeth. Although he could hear no sound he saw that she was screaming. Suddenly he dived into her body and was plunged into darkness. He could no longer see but could feel the body he was in. He felt pain and was overwhelmed by her agony. It cut through him. He opened his mouth and tried to scream but couldn't. The wave of torment momentarily subsided. Everything went calm, and he felt the soft kick of a baby in her belly. Before he had time to soak up this feeling, he was jerked out of its brief respite and racked by another wave of pain. It flowed through her entire body, but the source of her suffering was not the baby. Running through her body he sensed another affliction which he couldn't quite place. Before he had a chance to consider this he was wrenched back out of her body and became detached from it. Once again he was just an observer. He caught a good look at her face. It was familiar. He was shocked to recognise his mum.

....

Across the water Pidgin sat calmly on his ledge and watched Billy closely. Billy's eyelids fluttered rapidly and his body jerked. He rocked backwards and forwards on his knees, occasionally lifting himself off his haunches. His sneakers scraped on the rocks as his body snapped this way and that, producing a soft swishing sound. Every now and then he grunted faintly or muttered something to himself. An outside observer would have assumed that he was having some form of seizure. Apart from these muted sounds there was complete silence in the amphitheatre. Even the wind seemed to have stopped blowing.

....

The first image evaporated and was replaced by another. Following a bright flash of light, he saw the rising mushroom cloud of an atomic explosion. It immediately dissipated and was obscured by a burgeoning pall of black mist. His view swung from the growing mist to a clear view of the ground directly below him. He was hovering above an enormous crater filled with water. On the edge he could make out a small group of people. It was a family consisting of two adults and two children. They were accompanied by three dogs. Around the crater he could see a number of animal corpses. The bodies fanned out in all directions. His attention was drawn to a rising cloud of dust in the distance. It was trailing a line of motor vehicles which were heading directly towards the crater. Suddenly he was blinded by water gushing in his face. The flow stopped as suddenly as it started and he realised he was looking through someone else's eyes. They were looking at themselves in a full length mirror. He was in the body of another woman. She was naked, and cowered against a white, tile wall. Her fear was palpable. It permeated him to the point that he feared for his own life. His heart beat faster.

There was a sudden flash of light and he looked at his hands. However, they were not his hands. These hands were calloused and tough, not soft and manicured like his own. A heavy chain with large links lay across them. There was a sudden jerk on the chain and he felt as if he were choking. He gripped it with both hands and was dragged forward. His eyes followed the now taut chain. It ran up the back of a naked Aboriginal man and was attached to his neck. The carrier of the chain swung his head around. He opened his mouth to yell. Billy saw the butt of a rifle descend towards the man's head and with it a sheet of darkness.

Again there was a bright flash and suddenly he was underground. He watched a teenager crawling on his stomach through a tunnel. The tunnel was tight and claustrophobic, and the boy stopped for a moment and began scraping at its walls. Another flash and he was looking down on a huge gathering of people. He pulled up and away from the scene. There were pockets of people bunched in small groups around campfires. One fire was especially large and a group of men danced wildly around it. He was swamped by happiness. A smile spread across his face.

Peering down at Billy from the ledge Pidgin imitated him. His beard parted to expose a set of bright white teeth with a centre incisor missing.

There was another flash followed by pitch darkness. Billy heard the sound of approaching horses' hoofs, pounding on soft sand. There was a lot of screaming and a peculiar, acrid smell. It was if someone was having a barbecue but had splashed too much fuel on the fire. The smell bit into his nostrils. He choked on his own bile and involuntarily coughed. He grunted and cleared his throat. Overwhelming sorrow swept over him. It took his breath away.

There was a final, bright flash of light and Billy's eyes snapped open involuntarily. At first he saw nothing. His chest heaved and tears streamed down his face. They rolled off his chin, the droplets falling between his knees, slapping the rocks and raising small puffs of dust. He struggled vainly to calm himself before relenting and giving in to the feeling. He lurched forward onto his hands and knees. He curled his hands into fists, scraping his nails on the rocky floor. He arched his spine and drew back his head. A low whine rose in his throat, slowly growing in pitch and volume before unleashing itself as a bloodcurdling howl. It echoed off the circumjacent cliff faces and reverberated savagely back at him. It battered him on all sides. Incredible pain racked his body. He felt the agony of thousands of people, all crying out at once. He felt their fear and hardship. He was overwhelmed.

After a moment the feeling subsided and his head dropped forward. Most of the sorrow flowed out of him. He was relieved to let it go, although it didn't completely desert him. Some of it lingered. It gnawed at his chest. His hearing slowly tuned in to the sound of his own weeping, which brought him back from his semi-dream state. He sobbed loudly a few times and then stopped. There was only the sound of a gentle breeze in the trees. It hissed through the leaves and he heard the call of a solitary galah in the distance. Billy took a deep breath. He breathed in through his nose and choked on snot. He savagely spat it out and switched to breathing through his mouth. A calm gradually settled over him. He opened his eyes and stared down at his teardrops in the dust before raising himself up and sitting back on his haunches.

He looked across the water to the cliff face in front of him. The wall of stone was almost completely covered in handprints. The hands themselves were in the negative: they weren't painted but were outlined in a spray of red ochre. There must have been the prints of several generations on the wall. Pidgin was nowhere to be seen.

Billy gingerly stood and dusted off his knees. In complete silence and still in a trance he walked away from the waterhole and retraced his steps down the hill and back to the town. All the while he had the feeling that someone was behind him. He could almost feel their warm breath on his neck and felt as if eyes were burning a hole between his shoulder blades. He didn't dare look back.

Upon reaching the cabin he was totally exhausted and could barely walk. He was thankful that the town was so quiet and that he hadn't encountered anyone. He couldn't face talking to anyone. He needed time to process everything.

With some difficulty he opened the door and went inside, dragging it shut behind him with a satisfying click. For a moment he leant against the door, unsure where he was. He scanned the room and took some consolation in its familiarity. His eyes settled on the bed. He went directly to it and climbed in, clothes and all. He pulled the blanket up over his head, leaving a small gap through which to breathe. He closed his eyes and almost immediately fell into a deep sleep. His slumber was punctuated with the same vivid images he had seen at the waterhole. No one disturbed him and it was the following morning before he awoke.

THE CHURCH

Billy stared at the photograph. It was just like looking in the mirror. The face in the middle of the picture was practically his own. He checked his reflection in an adjacent window before looking at it again. Even the eyes of the subject in the photo were strangely familiar. They jumped out at him and everything else around them blurred.

The photo was old, very old. It was fading and two of its opposing edges were curling up out of its frame. It was mounted on a wall that evidently received a lot of sunlight. A broad yellow line ran through the centre of the photo where it had caught the most sun. Under the curled edges it still maintained the full spectrum of black, white and grey. At the moment it rested in the shadows. The sun had not yet fully illuminated the room.

Billy had hitched a ride with Rob to a slightly larger community further down the main road. He said he had some errands to run and had set Billy down near an old missionary church. He told him to have a look around. The place seemed deserted and Billy had invited himself inside through the open front doors. It was late in the morning and the heat of the day hadn't yet taken hold. The interior of the church was cool, almost like a cave, built as it was from solid stone. Fine dust played in the growing streams of sunlight filtering through its stained-glass windows.

In the photo were four figures, a man, a woman and two children, a boy and a girl. The girl was very young, about three years of age. She held onto the woman's hand and looked up at her. The woman looked back down at her. The boy was on his knees, playing in the sand with a short stick. The man was the only one looking at the camera. He wasn't just looking; he was staring. He glared straight down the barrel of the lens and through the portrait maker. It was unnerving. Billy had a curious feeling that the man was looking straight at him. He self-consciously looked behind himself to check that no one was standing behind him. He was alone.

The man wore an enormous grin. He exuded happiness and his smile was infectious. Billy invol-

untarily emulated the smile and a grin cut across
his face. He checked the reflection of this new pose
in the window. The resemblance was uncanny. He
peered deeper into the picture and could just make
out the outline of another figure behind the family.
It was barely discernible, just the outline of a human shape. It blended into the trees in the background. Only one feature stood out, and that was a
long, flowing beard. Billy blinked and refocused but
the figure wasn't any clearer. He couldn't be certain
if it was a trick of the light and the shadows of the
trees, or if there was really a fifth person in the portrait. The intense staring hurt his eyes and he relaxed his gaze. He massaged his eyes with the backs
of his hands.

The photograph made Billy consider what he
had. All the trappings he had left at home seemed
to have little worth now. The people in the picture
clearly had very little. Just the basics; not even
clothing. However, they appeared to be entirely
content. The man's smile confirmed this. Over the
past days Billy had adapted to similar conditions.
He had shed all his belongings, except for the
clothes on his back. He no longer had to contend
with the day-to-day pressures of the city. He didn't
even feel the urge to go back. He wondered what he
had been doing all the time down there anyway.

There didn't seem any point to it all. Take one day at a time. He didn't need more. He had enough right where he was.

He scrutinised the photo closely again. This time he focused on the woman. Billy caught his breath. He knew her. He was certain she was the same woman he had seen in his vision at the waterhole. The woman in the mirror, racked by fear. However, unlike the image in his head, she was untroubled, relaxed and serene. He was unsure if he was looking at the same person. He became confused, questioning his own sanity. What was going on? Who were these people? He looked again. There seemed to be a family resemblance, not only to the man but also the girl. She reminded him of the photos he had seen of his mother. He could barely remember her in real life. The only physical evidence he had of her were a few photographs. He had no real, firsthand experience of her. He again regretted knowing so little about her. He looked around the photo for a caption or explanation of who the people were. There was nothing. He moved around the room and looked at the other photos. There was quite a collection. Some had dates, mostly from the early nineteen thirties, but they provided no clue as to who the people posing in them were. Eventually he was drawn back to the first one. He stood and stared at it for a long time. He made a mental note to ask Doug about it the next time he saw him. Maybe he could provide some answers.

Where was everyone? Was Rob going to return?

Billy had moved outside and was sitting under the trees next to the church when a beaten-up Ford Cortina drove up and broke his contemplative silence. It slid to an abrupt halt in front of Billy and the billow of dust filing in its wake caught up to it and swirled around him. As it slowly settled the driver cranked down his window. It squealed in protest.

'Hi, I'm Wally.'

He swung open his door and climbed out of the car. He was tall and gaunt and stepped purposefully up to Billy. He extended his hand. Billy shook it reservedly. Who was this? His face was heavily swollen on one side. The injury looked very recent.

'I'm Billy,' he said.

'Have you been check'n out the museum?'

'Museum?'

Wally threw a thumb towards the church. 'Yeah, used to be a church. Now we're try'n to collect a bit of history from the area and put it on show.'

'Oh,' said Billy, 'and the people in the photos? Are they all from around here?'

'Most of 'em, although we've got people from all over here. Missionaries brought 'em in. They're also the ones who took the photos. There's someone managing it, but he's not around today. You'd have to come back another day if you wanna know more.'

'Thanks, I might do that.'

Wally fell silent for a minute. 'Look, I met you in the pub the other day. Well, at least, so I've been told.'

Billy thought he looked familiar but couldn't quite place him. 'Really?'

'I owe you an apology.'

'Is that so?'

'Kinda lost my head the other night.'

A pang of fear ran through Billy. This was his assailant. He cautiously took a step backwards. It dawned on him that he may have come to finish what he had started.

Wally noticed his apprehension. 'It's ok, I'm not gonna hurt you. I just kinda lose it when I get on the booze.'

'I'm waiting for someone, a guy called Rob. He was supposed to pick me up.'

Upon the mention of Rob's name Wally averted his gaze. 'Sorry, I don't know him.'

Billy suspected this wasn't the truth but decided to let it go. Even so, another troubling thought entered his head. He wondered if Rob had been the person that had rearranged Wally's face.

'Look, if you need a lift somewhere, I'd be more than willing to help you out. It'd be the least I could do considering what happened.'

Billy took a moment to mull over the offer. He had been waiting a long time and had begun to doubt that Rob would return. This community was even less familiar to him than where he was staying, and he didn't want to risk having to spend the night in yet another strange place.

'Ok, thanks for the offer. I need to get to a little town further down the road.'

'No worries. I know where you need to go. In you get then.'

Billy thought it strange that Wally knew so much about him but decided to go with the flow. He walked around the front of the car and sat in the passenger seat. Wally climbed in next to him. The car spluttered to life and Wally gunned the engine and threw the Cortina into gear. It lurched forward. He steered in a wide arc around the church square, raising a substantial cloud of dust behind them. Billy gripped the armrest on his door with both hands until his knuckles whitened. He began to doubt the little trust he had placed in Wally. Billy searched for his seatbelt, secured himself as best he could and steeled himself for the ride. Wally flashed him a sly grin and then pointed the vehicle onto a street leading away from the church. They cruised out of town.

....

The blanket of dust made its way into the church, rolling through the open front doors. Some of it came to settle on the photo that had captured Billy's attention. The smile on the man's face dissipated and appeared to fade to a blank look under the newly created film of dust.

KOPPARRAMURRA

....

1891

We knew that many tribes would be gathering at the market at Kopparramurra in the coming season. Due to the rains there would be good supplies of pituri and we would be able to exchange it for ochre if we made the trip past the great lakes and towards the mines at Bookatoo. Both these substances are very important to our ceremonies. We use pituri for coping with injuries and helping us see beyond this world. We usually chew it but I have known of others who smoke it. It is important that we trade for it directly with the Dieri. They are its custodians and only the most experienced of their elders, those with white beards, know how to harvest and prepare it properly. The ochre is important for a great many things, not least of which is giving our tribesmen a proper burial when the time arrives. It was to be an arduous journey and we would have to obtain enough supplies to last through difficult times, which would surely come again.

It had been the first good wet season for a long time. Before it had arrived, the Zebra Finch and the Pigeon had heralded its coming. They signal that a change is approaching and only come out to play when the scent of rain is in the air. Now that it was here flocks of budgerigars had infused new and bright colour into the homelands. Even though I had seen it before I marvelled at the transformation that took place in our homelands. Animals and plants sprang to life out of the once parched earth. It was a wonderful sight. Even fish woke from their sandy beds. It was as if the land was celebrating with everything it had to offer. Unfortunately, we knew that the wet wouldn't last long. The rains had turned the desert around us into enormous lakes. Once the rain ceased the lakes would disappear as quickly as they had been formed. The desert would swallow them up once again. We could not be complacent and needed to make preparations for the hard times which would surely follow. Already the rains were becoming intermittent. All the tribes knew this and we were taking this opportunity to trade while supplies were still in abundance.

I had set out with several of my fathers and brothers. We made sure that we had the right message sticks to guarantee safe passage through hostile territory. In the past we would have travelled in a much larger group but we had a lost a great many warriors and this was no longer possible. It had become our responsibility to ensure supplies for our family. The size of our group meant that we would not be able to carry as much as we had in the past. We still hoped that we could secure enough supplies to last until the next rains. The most prized ochre lay far beyond the great salt lake and came from the blood of the sacred emu. The journey to the mine itself was a long one. Even so, we had decided it was more profitable to mine it ourselves and not to trade for it further from the source. There was some degree of risk. We had heard rumours that the mine may no longer be accessible, and perhaps had even been taken over by the invaders. There was uncertainty as to whether anyone could mine there at all. If so this would be a great disappointment. The ochre from Bookatoo was unequalled in quality. There were other sources, but nothing came close to it in terms of colour and purity.

Upon arrival our fears were thankfully unfounded and we were relieved to find the custodians still guarding the mines. We remained wary of the presence of the invaders, although some of them had become our friends and could be trusted. Not all of them were bad. We had established good relationships with many of them. There were those among them who respected our traditions and allowed us to freely use our lands as we always had. We had recently made contact with those who appeared to be wise men from their tribe. They were learning our language and we were learning some of theirs. These men seemed to be very interested in the way we lived and appeared to be studying us. I was fairly certain their motives are honourable. This was at odds with some of the others we had encountered.

When I was younger I witnessed enormous brutality on their part, mainly led by one of their lawmen. Willshire was his name. Mercifully, his killing ways were being curbed. One of their wise men, who went by the name of Gillen, had come to our aid. The problem lay not solely with Willshire, for there were many more like him. And there did not appear to be enough Gillens to hold them all at bay.

The threat from the invaders was not the only problem we faced. We needed to be back home within a couple of seasons as there was a new batch of apprentices who would need to go through final initiation. Many ceremonies would have to be performed. I had made the trip once before with my birth father to the markets but never to the mines. This time my father had taken ill from a spear wound and needed time to recover. Due to the recent rains the going was tough. Much of our journey involved traversing the wide lakes which had appeared. We still had one experienced guide who knew the route even though the landscape had changed. We did not have to worry about the abundance of food, although finding clean water did present a problem at times. We had taken with us a quantity of our best spears and boomerangs, as well as hair string which we hoped would be in high demand.

Mining was hard work. It was dark and cramped. Fortunately I was small enough to wriggle deep down into the depths. It felt as though I was travelling into the bowels of our mother, the earth. I feared the spirit that lived there and had asked permission to enter. Even so, I felt that I didn't have much time. I wasn't willing to anger the spirit. I was, after all, a guest in this place. There came a point when I couldn't see my own hands. It was darker than a starless night. My uncle had taught me how to make a small fire and I lit it on a loose rock. After some searching I found the vein of ochre. I had been told that it would be easy to spot.

There was clearly still a great deal to be mined. This was indeed a resource which would not conceivably be extracted before the end of time.

I had a stone tool for which we had bartered earlier on our journey, but most of the time it was easier with my hands. I sat cross-legged and hunched over in order to scrape away the rock. I was relieved that several large blocks fell away and I placed them in my dish. Once it was full I extinguished my fire and slid back down the tunnel, pushing the food dish in front of me. As I went I kept knocking my head on the jagged roof above me. By the time I reached the entrance my hair was smeared with blood and dirt. I gave my uncles quite a scare when I emerged. They thought I was the spirit coming out of the mine to punish them. I tried to maintain the illusion but I couldn't help laughing at their reaction and this gave me away.

I crawled deep into the mine several times until we had as much as we could carry. In the meantime my uncles prepared the ochre for travel. They ground it down to fine paste and made large balls by mixing it with water. At one end of each of the balls they formed an indentation so that we could carry it on our heads. I marvelled at its colour. It shone bright red and sparkled in the sunlight. It was truly beautiful. I realised how precious it was and why we had made such an arduous journey to obtain it.

Before leaving we spent some time thanking the spirit for allowing us to mine. We also presented the caretakers of the mine with two of our best spears and the tools we had bartered for. We then began our return journey, back towards the lakes.

It was only later when we were at the markets that we became aware how fortunate we had been. We were told that the invaders had been there since we left and killed a number of the caretakers. We did not know if we would ever be able to return there in the future. I felt honoured that I had been given the opportunity to go there, and even more so that I had been chosen to enter the mine. I was certain the memories of the experience would always remain with me.

The market was extremely busy. I don't think I had ever seen so many people gathered in one place. There must have been hundreds of men. My fathers had feared that there wouldn't be many people, but it was clear their fears were unfounded. We set up camp and started our fire. The atmosphere was incredibly jovial. There was much discussion about the situation with the invaders. Many tribes told stories similar to ours. A great many people had been slaughtered. Some of the tribes from where the sun rises spoke proudly of dealing out retribution for the killings, but they were the exception. For the most part, people were fearful of evoking the rage of the invaders. Many held strong to the view that one day soon these brutal men would tire of our land and return to where they came from. Personally I doubted this. I was sure the invaders were here to stay and that things would get worse before they got better. There was also much discussion about members of tribes who had gone to work for the invaders. It seemed that not all the invaders were bad, but those who could be trusted and provide something worthwhile for our labours were few and far between. A lot of warriors were against helping the invaders at all and felt that those who went to work for them were being exploited. There was a lot of talk about mistreatment of the womenfolk, and in particular women who had been taken as partners by the invaders. Many were concerned that this undermined our marriage system. There were complaints from warriors who had been promised in a marriage to particular women and were having to deal with their being claimed by invaders. Many of these situations had ended violently, I was told, with casualties on both sides. There was great fear of the incredible force of the invaders' weapons. These were difficult times indeed.

Eventually all had been said that could be said on the subject of the invaders and the mood lightened greatly. Food was shared. A fine delicacy was the fish which we only rarely saw and only came with the rains. As night fell we all took to dancing and singing. A lot of new stories I didn't know were performed and the celebrations went deep into the night. What a fine evening that was. We were swept back to a time when things were a lot simpler. To a time when we respected one another and the rules were clear. I feared for what lay ahead and it saddened me to think that perhaps a night like this wouldn't happen ever again, at least not on such a grand scale.

The following morning we had a bite to eat and set about bartering. There were all manner of goods to be had, but our plan was already fixed. We threw down a portion of our ochre and waited for a reasonable bid. Eventually a good supply of pituri was offered, although we did have to sweeten the deal with some hair string. We now had all that we could possibly carry and a generous supply for the coming time. It was with some relief and with less trepidation that we embarked on our journey home.

SIX

·······································

SERIOUS BUSINESS

THE INTERVENTION

Wally had dropped Billy off on the dirt road leading to the community and just within sight of it. Then, without saying a word, he had thrown the car into gear, swung it around and roared off back towards the main road. Billy watched him go and shielded his face with in the crook of his elbow against the cloud of dust that engulfed him. He held his breath until it settled. He then turned and walked the last few hundred metres towards the town. The sun was ferocious and he laboured under its heat.

For a great deal of the drive back to the community Wally and Billy had sat in silence. His former attacker had maintained his focus on the road and not made any attempt to instigate a conversation. Billy had thought it best just to let him be. The apologies had been made and there didn't seem to be anything further to discuss. At one point they were forced to talk, though. Wally had slammed on the brakes without warning and sent Billy flying forward in his seatbelt. The belt had cut deep into his neck and the force of it jarring against his chest had taken the wind out of him. Billy had cursed and thrown an angry look at him. Wally had nonchalantly lifted a hand and pointed through the windscreen.

'Emu,' he said.

Billy peered through the dirty glass and saw the tall, awkward-looking bird loping slowly off into the scrub on the side of the road. It blended very well with its surroundings and was quite difficult to spot. Had he not known it was there he would have been oblivious to its presence.

'They always travel in twos,' said Wally.

Sure enough, a moment later a second emu cantered gracefully out of the bush, crossed the road in front of the car and made off after its partner.

'They're my totem. It's up to me to protect them,' said Wally.

'Oh?'

'Yeah, it's my responsibility to make sure they are killed and cooked in the right way. Out here when you're born you get given a totem.'

'So you can't eat emu, then?'

'Nah, it's not like that. I'm sorta more of a care-taker.'

'Oh, I see.'

Billy didn't fully understand but felt uncomfort-able pressing for more information. He was still finding it difficult to talk to him because of their previous altercation. Wally focussed back on the road ahead and didn't seem to want to elaborate anyway. He put the Cortina back in first gear and slowly accelerated. As he did so, he peered through the cars grimy side windows and made sure there was no other wildlife waiting to spring out of the scrub. Once satisfied, he settled back into his seat, planted his foot on the accelerator and returned to staring blankly through the windscreen. They lis-tened to the roar of the badly tuned engine for the remainder of the journey.

Billy stopped and wiped his brow. He had made swift progress along the road towards the town. The sun was beating down relentlessly upon him and he had pushed on in order to get out of it as soon as possible. He inspected the sweat on the back of his hand. It had turned black from mixing with the red dust. He continued on and had reached the outskirts of the community when he heard a woman's high-pitched yell. 'No!'

A glint of metal in the sun caught his eye. Just off the main road was a small clearing between the dried-out gum trees. Rob's Ford was parked in the middle of the clearing. It looked almost as if it had been abandoned. It appeared as if the car had careened off the road as it was heading into town. There were deep crevices in the bulldust on the side of the road where the tyres had slewed into the dirt. Billy felt uneasy. It looked as though the driver had lost control and just managed to avoid hitting the trees before the car had come to rest.

As he approached, Billy could see that the driver's door was slightly ajar and the interior light was on. He could make out a pair of shadows struggling in the front seat. The car was rocking gently on its suspension. Billy cautiously approached. He recognised Rob spread out across the seat with his back to him. He appeared to be doing push-ups. Rob stopped, sat back up on his knees and seemed to be trying to force something down. Billy was standing next to the driver's door and could now see clearly into the car's interior. A pair of bare legs was spread around Rob's waist. They were kicking and thrashing. Over Rob's right shoulder Billy recognised Mabel's face. Her teeth were gritted and she was covered in sweat. He saw an odd mixture of rage and fear in her eyes. She saw Billy and the anger took over.

'Get off me, you arsehole!'

Billy was nailed to the spot and watched as she opened her mouth to scream. Before she could utter a sound Rob slapped his wide, right hand across her mouth and forced her head down against the seat. Billy was uncertain what to do. Clearly Mabel was not a willing party to this. For a moment he hesitated, trying to decide if he should intervene. He was torn between the affection he felt for his new-found friend and this situation. He was not really a part of their world and was confused about his role in it. So many strange and new things had happened that he doubted if he had the right to intervene. But deep down he was horrified by what was going on. One human being was attacking another. It didn't matter where they were. This was not right.

Billy gripped the door handle and pulled. It refused to respond. This surprised him as the door was slightly open. He grimaced and cursed. The damn doors on this rust bucket! He tried again, this time using both hands and all of his strength. The door swung open with a loud squeal and Billy stumbled backwards, landing squarely on his arse. Rob spun around in surprise. Seeing Billy he opened his mouth to speak but no sound came out. He sprang from the car, surprisingly fast for such a tall man, and in one deft movement holstered his now flaccid weapon and zipped up his pants. He stood over Billy and reached out his hand, making an attempt to diffuse the situation. 'What y' doing down there? Hav'n a dirt bath?'

Billy was astounded by Rob's flippancy. 'I think I should be asking you that question.'

'Just hav'n a bitta fun.'

'Didn't look like it was reciprocated.'

'Huh?'

Billy rephrased with irritation, 'It didn't look like both of you we're enjoying yourselves.'

He stood up and dusted off his jeans. Stepping around Rob and purposefully avoiding looking at him, he moved to the side of the car. Softly he called out to Mabel and inquired how she was. She didn't respond and cowered in the far corner of the front seat, hard up against the passenger's side door. Her chin against her chest, she looked timidly up at him from under her eyebrows. She was shaking violently. He reached into the car and gently beckoned her out. She shrank back further into her corner. He smiled at her and reached out his hand.

'It's ok, you're safe now,' he said.

She studied his eyes for a moment. Upon registering that he was genuine she let her body relax. She slid across the seat and cautiously took his hand. He helped her out of the car and together they turned to face Rob. There was a moment of silence. Nobody moved and it felt like a standoff.

Rob was simmering. Billy saw the rage boiling up in him and could see this was not going to end well. He gently coaxed Mabel behind him, using himself as a human shield. Billy felt her grasp his arm. Digging her nails into it she sneered at Rob, 'Fuck you.'

Rob ignored her, focussed solely on Billy.

'What do you think you're doin'? Eh? This is none of your business. That bitch is one of ours.'

Billy grimly held his ground. Rob exploded.

'Fuck you,' he screamed and lunged forward with his right arm, his fist in a tight ball.

Time slowed almost to a stop for Billy. He saw the fist approaching but was riveted to the spot and felt powerless to move. Suddenly an outside force propelled him sideways. He felt his sneakers sliding across the sand but he wasn't the driving force. Over Rob's shoulder he could just make out a figure half blended with the trees. It was Pidgin. At first Billy was startled. He then stood mesmerised as his entire body went numb. It was as if he was paralysed and having an out of body experience. He no longer had control of his body and was an innocent and helpless bystander. He saw the fist approaching and even felt the wind it created, caressing his cheek as it flew by. Rob quickly adjusted his aim and threw another punch. Again Billy's body slid sideways and just out of range. Rob stopped. Panting, he straightened his back. Time for Billy accelerated back up to normality. He stared down at his body. He felt power returning to his limbs. He wiggled his fingers and toes to test that they were indeed his to control again. He exhaled softly through pursed lips, took a deep breath and waited for Rob's next move. He peered over his shoulder and into the scrub but could no longer see his silent saviour. Rob let his shoulders slump and dropped his hands. Billy composed himself and turned to Mabel. 'C'mon, let's go.'

Rob contemplated stopping them but looked defeated and could only manage a half-hearted, 'C'mon, mate.'

Billy ignored him. Mabel was still shaking and obviously in pain. She could barely walk. He slung an arm around her waist and together they hobbled back to the road and towards the town. Billy could feel Rob's piercing stare drilling a hole between his shoulderblades. He resisted the urge to look back.

WOMENS BUSINESS

Doris sat Billy at the kitchen table. With slow deliberation, she made them both a cup of tea and sat in front of him. He cupped his hands around the warm mug and tried to settle himself. He stared at a few loose tea leaves circling around in the milky concoction. He looked up and met Doris's gaze across the table. He could see a mix of pain and compassion in her eyes.

'Are you ok?'

'Kind of.'

'The other women will take care of her.'

He nodded slowly.

'What will happen to him, to Rob?'

'I dunno. It's up ta the men to decide that. They'll know what to do with him. It might take a bitta time, though. Doug has been called and he's on his way from Alice.'

'There's a phone here?'

'Of course there is. We're not completely isolated, you know. There's one in the town office opposite the store.'

Billy was taken aback. 'Really?'

'Yep, why? Do you need to call someone?'

'No, not anymore. Shouldn't we call the police though?'

'Not right now. What can they do anyway? It's for us to decide what to do. If necessary we'll let 'em know later. We have our own punishments. We've had a lot of trouble dealing with their law and ours. They're two very different systems. In the past they'd first make decisions according to their laws. It was only later on that we'd have the opportunity to settle the case our way, if at all. It's our people, our law. Either way, our punishment has to be carried out otherwise the case won't be closed. This time we've decided to do it the right way around.'

Doris paused. Sensing that more of an explanation was necessary, she continued, 'In the old days, we women had our secret stuff and magic and the men had theirs. It was forbidden to know the men's business. If a woman saw something she wasn't supposed to, it could mean death. Also men had certain rights over the women in the tribe. What just happened might have been allowed under certain circumstances. I won't say that we were exploited, but for the good of the tribe there were occasions when it was expected that we give favours. That was a long time ago, though. Now things are different; but because of us having two laws to abide by, the white man's and our own, things are also much more complicated.'

'But rape is not right.'

'I agree, and you did the right thing stopping him, Billy. What happened has no connection with traditional law. It's just plain wrong. In the past everyone knew what was expected of them. We knew what'd happened if we didn't follow the law. We accepted it. Things were just the way they were. In some ways life was simpler. The rules were clearer. You see, it works like this. There are three things: the law, the land and the people. They're all linked. If you break the law, the land and the people suffer. You can't hurt one without affecting the others. That's why it's so important that Rob faces punishment for what he's done.'

Billy nodded slowly before straightening in his chair. 'I'm guessing he's gone. What if they can't find him?'

'Don't worry, the men will find him. It's in their hands now. If he has any sense he will know he has to face up to what he's done and won't shy away from the consequences. He's a good boy and I'm having trouble understanding why this has happened. I think alcohol played a part in it.'

'Yes, it could have been. I smelt it on his breath.'

Doris sighed and looked down at her cup, a troubled look on her face. Billy lent back in his chair and rested his fingertips on the edge of the table. He took a deep breath and tried to relax. This had been a lot for him to take in all at once. He was struggling to understand the intricacies of their law and wondered what the punishment would be. He realised it was important to let these people deal with their own. However, he didn't completely agree that the police should be kept out of it. A crime had been committed. Yet, because of the people involved, it was very difficult for him to keep an open mind. Someone he had just begun to get to know had done something terrible. Before this happened he had felt that they were forming a friendship. Now he didn't know what to think about Rob. And why did the victim have to be Mabel of all people? She had been kind to him as well, and although he didn't really know her, he thought they had also been building a rapport. Two of the people who had helped him begin to connect with this place had somehow been taken away. He felt deserted. On the other hand, through this turn of events, he was suddenly a sort of honorary member of the community. He wasn't sure if that was what he really wanted. He was also disturbed by what would happen to Rob once they got hold of him.

'What will they do with him if they find him?'

'The men will decide.' Doris studied his face. 'Maybe I should tell you a bit about how things used to be. Now it would seem quite rough, maybe even ... What's the word? Barbaric. In the old days we had laws for a reason. They protected us. There was no other way.'

She sipped on her tea.

'I remember when I was a child, Doug was really sick. He was lying on the ground and not moving. Someone called for the spiritual man and he came. I watched him do the healing, even though it wasn't allowed. The spiritual man came out of the bushes and began searching Doug's body for something. He then stood up and leapt into a nearby bush.'

She half stood at the table and mimicked diving sideways. Puffing from the sudden exertion she eased herself slowly back into her chair.

'He came back out with something carefully cupped in his hands. He bent over Doug and re-turned what was in his hands into Doug's body. It was his soul. Our beliefs explain that all sickness occurs when the soul departs the body. The further the soul is away from the body, the sicker the patient.'

She held the cup of tea in front of her and ran one finger over the contour of the handle.

'The next day Doug was better, walking 'round just like nothing had happened. Nobody knew I was there, which was lucky. They probably would have killed my mother because of it. I was her responsibility, and she let me see these things, so she would have been punished, even if she wasn't aware that I had been there. I guess that's pretty harsh, but like I said we knew the law and what would happen if we disobeyed it. It's all about respect.'

She looked up from her cup and across at Billy. 'I'm sorry. I suppose I've been going on a bit.'

'No, really. It's fine.'

She scanned his face carefully. Satisfied that he was genuine, she gave him a reassuring smile. 'Good. I think it's important you know why we do things a certain way. It might help if you understand a bit about how we had to live. Everything we had came from the land. There were good and bad seasons. Most of the time we women had to provide for everyone. We knew where food was in the ground and usually could depend on it. Sometimes the men would kill some meat—kangaroo or something—but hunting didn't provide a lot of food. Generally it was up to us.'

A broad smile cut across her face and she chuckled. 'You know those men like to think they were running the show, but hey, they would've been lost without us.'

She stopped for a moment and the smile slipped away and her face darkened. 'Having kids was also pretty difficult. If you gave birth to twins, which happened sometimes, there'd usually be a weaker one. In that case the weaker one would be killed. The same would go for someone who was too sick to care for. It was all about survival. We didn't have very much out here in the desert, so anyone who put extra pressure on our resources was a problem. It could be very costly for the whole tribe. They were hard decisions, but in the end you had to do what was best for everyone concerned. Now there are taboos that prevent such things happening, mainly based on Christian morals. I dunno what's better, keeping someone alive artificially with medicine or letting nature take its course. In the old days we didn't have the luxury of such choices.'

She paused and lent forward over her tea cup. Her voice softened. 'In the past if someone died, we would bury them and stay away from their place. Now if someone dies we clear out their house, give it a bit of time to settle and their spirit time to leave. Then we repaint the house, give it a bit of a makeover. Then someone else can move in. We don't mention the dead. We leave them be.'

Billy was so deeply engrossed in her stories that he sat bolt upright when there was a knock at the front door and someone pushed the screen door open. It screeched loudly on its hinges. It was Doug. He stood in the doorway, his body blocking out the sunlight.

'We've found him,' he said.

BOGGY HOLE

....

1886

We had been camping away from the men for some days with the mothers, brothers and sisters. It was to be a great occasion. My brother was to be initiated. He was off in another camp with all the men, preparing for the ceremony. I was too young to participate. It would be a few seasons before I would begin the process of becoming a man. What I saw that day would stay with me for the rest of my days. It would also be a lesson I wish I had never learnt. Our homeland was no longer ours, and ours alone. We would have to share it with the invaders whether we liked it or not.

It was early morning. Our camp was silent and there was a fine mist in the air from our smouldering fires. The sun cast long shadows through the trees. As usual at this time of the morning, the air had a bitter-cold, biting edge. The heat of the day was yet to encroach into the camp and take over from the warmth of the dying fires.

We were woken by their approach. Because we slept with our ears to the bare ground, we heard everything. Especially something that reverberated with such force. The pounding of the horses' hooves was unmistakable. The earth shook. I had once thought a horse to be a large dog and feared it not only for its size, but especially because of its teeth. I now know better. I now know that the horses are not to be feared as much as the men that ride on them. They are capable of such evil deeds that the mind is unable to comprehend. For a long time we had been able to defend ourselves but times had changed. They now had a new weapon called a Martini-Henry. It spat magic fire and a kind of stone. I had overheard that it could be used to kill very large wild animals. An elephant, they said. I don't know what an elephant is but I can only assume it must be much bigger than a kangaroo. In any case, I had no doubts regarding its purpose. It was an efficient killing machine and had the ability to fell more than one warrior with a single stone.

Long before they were in the camp they started firing these weapons. I was not yet fully awake and somewhat disorientated. We were all taken by surprise. Normally the older men would have been there to defend us, but on this day, because of the ceremonies, this was not the case. I suspect the invaders took this moment to attack because our camp had been split.

There was an incredible amount of noise and commotion in the camp. Everything was in disarray. All around me my mothers were crying and whimpering. Some of the smaller children were screaming. I was on my feet at once and began frantically searching for an escape route. My sister had been lying next to me. She went to stand up and at once lay back down. Behind her two of my cousins also fell to the ground. Such was the power of this new weapon. It could extinguish three lives with a single stone. Blood poured from the side of her head and, although her body still twitched, I could see that her spirit was no longer of this world. I howled at the top of my lungs. I had lost one of my brothers not long ago in a similar attack. Thankfully I was not present when this had occurred, but the stories I had been told had severely shaken me. I looked down in distress at my sister. For a brief moment, a memory flashed across my mind of us playing together in the sand and searching for bush potatoes. We had always been close to one another and had done almost everything together. I was distraught that I had not been able to protect her. My sister had only seen the seasons cycle nine times.

More hot stones whistled past my ears. In the distance I saw an ever-expanding wall of men and horses bearing down on us. A cloud of dust rose up high behind them and it seemed for all the world as if they were descending from the sky. They were still quite a way off but it would not be long before they were upon our campsite. I forced my anguish aside. Spinning around, I leapt high over our campfire and made for the shelter of some nearby trees. On the way I seized the arm of one of my younger cousins. If I had known what was going to happen I would have tried to take more of my family with me. In retrospect, I expect I did the right thing. Otherwise it would probably have cost me my life. My cousin had not been walking for very long but was mercifully already a strong runner on his baby legs. I zigzagged as I had seen the emu do, dragging my cousin behind me all the while. I yelled at him to stay low to the ground and tried to make myself as small as possible, although it was difficult to run in this position. In the end I had to lift him from the ground. His little legs just weren't fast enough to compete with mine.

Behind me I could still hear the horses' hooves. Their clatter echoed loudly off the surrounding hills. I wasn't certain if they were already upon the camp and were now also chasing me down. In the chaos all my senses were being bombarded and I barely knew what was up and what was down. I did not dare turn around as it would slow our escape. I focussed only on a mound between the trees in the distance. A figure stood on the mound. At a distance it looked like a large bird, but strangely in the shape of a man. He seemed to be calling to me. I kept running until the sound from the camp had faded a little. By the time we reached the mound the figure was gone.

I found some shelter behind a large rock and pushed my cousin down into a small crevice between the underside of the rock and the sand. I motioned for him to stay completely still and tried to hide the parts of his body that were sticking out by heaping sand against him. In no time the only part showing was the bridge of his nose and his eyes. They filled me with fear, such was their intense, piercing stare. He began to cry and I could see the sand slowly changing colour around his eyes. In a moment he would run out of air and I quickly cleared the sand away from his mouth and nose. He exhaled softly. I watched the granules of sand shift with his breath. He stayed perfectly still. Even at his young age he was aware of the danger upon us. I tried to give him a reassuring smile but couldn't muster the strength. Only then did I attempt to see what was going on in the camp.

Without revealing myself, I found a small hole in one corner of the rock and by looking through it I could see most of what was happening. I was relatively certain that they could not see me. However, we were a good deal closer to the camp than I had expected. Even behind the rock I knew we would be discovered if they headed our way. I pulled some loose spinifex over myself but was sure that if they searched thoroughly, they would still find me.

The men were now in the camp and still on their horses. There was practically no one from my tribe left standing, apart from two of my mothers who cowered to one side in each other's arms. The men had stopped using their powerful weapons and were now busy with their swords. Two of them dismounted and proceeded to slash at the bodies on the ground. The other men trampled over them with their horses. I did not want to look but an anger rose in me and I could not avert my eyes. I wanted to see it all so that I could tell my fathers and grandfathers what had happened. The images of that day still reverberate in my head and sometimes I wish I had just taken my cousin and slipped away.

Eventually all the men dismounted. There must have been about ten of them. To my surprise I recognised some them to be from another tribe. They looked very different wearing the invaders coverings. They were all dressed in the uniform of their lawmen. They participated heartily in what was going on and didn't seem to show any remorse for their actions. I can only assume they were from a distant tribe. We had heard that from the place where the sun rose there were many like them. Warriors who would kill just for the fun of it; but also those who did it to protect their own people from suffering the same fate we were experiencing.

The camp had now become relatively silent. Then I heard the crying of a baby. I saw one of the men searching through the bodies and from among them he pulled out the child. He held it aloft by its legs and the other men broke out in laughter. I saw the man swing the baby over his shoulder and forward towards the ground. I closed my eyes, clenching my eyebrows inwards until the taut skin on the sides of my head hurt. I wanted to fold myself inwards and disappear. I heard a loud thump, and then another. The baby stopped crying. My heart pounded so hard I thought they would be able to hear it. I tried to calm myself by breathing slowly. I felt sick in my stomach and this feeling stayed with me for some time. I opened my eyes and looked down at my cousin. He saw the fear in my eyes and wriggled further down under the rock. I laid my hand softly on the sand over his body. It felt warm and helped me to relax somewhat.

I heard screaming and peered through the hole again. The men had gathered around my two mothers who had been holding each other. They seemed glued to spot. I was wishing they would run but they seemed incapable of doing anything, such was their fear. I couldn't see what was happening anymore as all the men surrounded them. In some way this was good, as I felt unable to absorb even the things I had already seen. For a long time the men were huddled over my mothers. I heard screaming and this continued for some time, before it suddenly stopped. The men then spread out but I could no longer see the women. After this the men seemed to be congratulating one another and took small containers out of their saddlebags and drank from them. Later they took large sacks from the horses and splashed some kind of liquid over the entire campsite. They then mounted their horses again. It seemed that one of them was in charge. Before they left this man lit a stick with fire and cast it onto the bodies. Flame erupted immediately from the ground and spread quickly across the campsite. I had never seen fire do this before. I now know this magic liquid is called kerosene. The man watched the flames for a short period and then motioned to his companions. They turned their horses and rode away from the campsite. I was thankful they had chosen to ride away from our hiding place as I was sure we would have been discovered otherwise.

I did not know the area where we camped very well as we were not normally allowed there. It was a sacred area for my mother and her sisters. Initiated men were not allowed there. Even so, I knew that eventually we would be missed and they would come looking for us. I decided to wait for my brother and father to return with the other men. There was not much else I could do. Somewhere among the bodies lay my own mother. I wanted to go to her and my sister but the fire burned with such ferocity that I didn't dare go near it. I could feel the heat of it from where I sat. I also feared that the men would return. We stayed where we were and I remained vigilant for the sound of horses' hoofs. I watched the fire burn. Sometimes the wind blew the smoke in our direction. We then had to cover our noses and mouths. It carried such a pungent odour. The day was ending when it finally went out by itself. My cousin and I stayed huddled together by the rock. That night it was very cold but we didn't dare make a fire or go look for water. We just held each other for warmth. I cannot recall that we even spoke to one another. Such was our shock. That day we learnt a new word—war.

The following morning we were found.

SEVEN

....

THE LAW

THE PUNISHMENT

Doug had invited Billy along but warned him that under normal circumstances only initiated men would be allowed to be present. He had told Billy to remain silent and keep out of the way. He explained that he thought it important that Billy see what was going on. They slowly climbed the track leading up to the waterhole in the foothills behind the community.

'We've had a long discussion about how we should deal with this,' he said. 'This is not the sort of behaviour we accept around here. Usually we would banish Rob from the camp, but we we're afraid that it would push him down the wrong path. Banishment is the ultimate punishment. In the past being exiled from your family was the equivalent of a death sentence.'

Billy listened but his mind was wandering. They were heading up to where he had seen Pidgin, and the images that had played out in his head still haunted him. He had returned to the community expecting to have a relaxing time but nothing could have been farther from the truth. The environment was far harsher than he had expected. Billy tried to focus on what Doug was saying. They were nearly at the entrance to the rockhole and were both panting from the heat and the exertion of the climb.

'He will still have to spend some time away from the camp and we will take him out into the desert for a while until he recovers. He will not be alone. It is important that he realises how crucial upholding the law is.'

Billy wondered what Rob would have to recover from, but as they reached the clearing next to the rockhole it soon became apparent that it was going to involve a good deal of pain.

In the cool shadows near the water's edge four men stood, all brandishing spears. The spears were about two metres long with wickedly jagged barbs at their pointed ends. Billy hadn't seen the men before. They seemed oblivious to his presence and focussed their attention on Doug. Doug motioned Billy to stay where he was before walking over to the small group of men. In low murmurs they acknowledged each other and discussed their next move. Abruptly they stopped talking and turned towards a sheer cliff face at the far end of the enclosure. Billy followed their gaze.

There Rob stood, alone. He was slightly bent over and cowering on the rocks, up against the cliff wall. He didn't move and his breathing was barely perceptible. He looked for all the world like a disobedient child who had been told to stand in the corner. Fear clouded his expression. It was clear that he was willing to accept his punishment but he was also aware of what it involved. It wasn't going to kill him but it was certainly going to hurt. He became aware that all attention had shifted to him and drew himself up to his full height. He flattened his back to the wall behind him and splayed out his hands to either side. Billy watched Rob's knuckles turn white as he gripped the rocks behind him. He dug his fingernails into the wall. He raised his head, gritted his teeth and bravely faced his accusers. The look of fear on his face melted away and an uneasy calm came over him. He didn't seem to notice Billy, or anyone else for that matter. His stare was fixed onto some point far in the distance.

For a moment nobody moved. It formed a strange tableau. Rob exposed and plastered to the wall, the men in a line with spears raised, and Billy standing solitary to one side. Then, as if on cue, one by one the men threw their spears. They kept their aim low. It was clear that they only wanted to strike his legs and didn't want to maim him permanently, although from his stance there was a good chance he could sacrifice his manhood. Rob grimaced in anticipation as each spear flew towards him. The spears flew past his legs, clattered off the cliff face, and fell harmlessly at his feet. Not one of them found their target.

Finally Doug stepped forward. He crouched low, stretched his arm back as far as it would it extend and threw his spear with all the force he could muster. For such a bulky man he moved with incredible agility. Billy had only ever seen him quietly seated or moving with slow deliberation. He was surprised to see him suddenly so active. The spear found its target. It buried itself deep into Rob's thigh, halfway between his knee and his crotch. He let out a high pitched scream and slumped to the ground, sliding along the cliff face as he went down. The spear remained lodged in his leg. The shaft slapped the rocks at his feet as Rob collapsed.

There was a short period of silence. Nobody moved and Rob appeared to have passed out. The men nodded to each other before walking over to where Rob lay and standing over his prostrate body.

Doug knelt beside him and closely examined his leg. He beckoned to the other men to help and together they picked up Rob and laid him out on his side and away from the cliff face. One of the men supported the spear. It had passed a good way through Rob's leg and the sight turned Billy's stomach. Doug indicated for the others to hold Rob down and then gripped the spear by its barbed end with both hands. He twisted it violently and wrenched it out. Rob's body twitched and the men tightened their grip on him. Doug had to thread almost the entire length of the shaft through the leg. It was clear the barbs would not pass through in reverse. He grunted as he worked. Close to the end he gave it one last yank and pulled it free. He nearly toppled over backwards in the process. One of the other men caught him before he fell.

Reverently they rolled Rob's body onto his back and stood aside.

Doug gingerly massaged own his lower back and quipped, 'Think I might've overdone it a bit.'

One of the other men shook his head. 'Gettin' old, mate?'

He then made a joke about hooking a small fish and that they should throw it back. There was a pregnant pause before they all burst spontaneously into laughter. The mood lightened significantly. Chuckling, Doug turned and walked across to Billy.

'Ok, show's over. Let's go. I could use a cuppa tea.'

Together they walked across the rocks. Billy looked back over his shoulder and saw that the men were preparing to treat Rob's wounds. They had a wooden dish and appeared to be mixing some sort of paste in it. Billy wanted to stay and watch but Doug continued to lead him away and beckoned him to follow.

Billy walked behind Doug to the exit of the natural amphitheatre. He noted that his entire back was coated in flies. As they entered the narrow passageway the wind began to whistle around his ears. He could have sworn it carried the sound of someone calling his name but he didn't dare look around. He focussed solely on the flies crawling across Doug's t-shirt.

BLACK AND WHITE

Aboriginal. Aborigine. Billy thought about the words. He wasn't sure which one was correct. It didn't matter. Neither of them was correct. Either way it was a word; it was about a thing. It described something but it wasn't human. It made it seem as if the people were just an object, not something that lived and breathed. It was belittling, another instrument to downplay their significance. It was an old word, antiquated and from another time. Every nation and culture in the world had their own dedicated name. An Englishman was an Englishman, a German was a German. Why was it that these people weren't given the same respect? Why not just call them what they were? They were all from different tribes, the Pitjantjatjara, Arrernte, Yankunytjatjara and so forth. So they should be named as such. But what was he? He needed to find that out, but how? He knew very little about his mother, only that her tribe had been dispersed, the language and culture lost. All of it systematically destroyed and wiped from the face of the planet. It was extinct. But animals that were considered extinct have sometimes re-emerged. There were still sightings of the Tasmanian tiger. So there was some hope. He knew in himself that he was something, only it didn't have a name. At the very least, maybe the people of the community would accept him and then he would know what to call himself.

It seemed that balance was necessary. The old and the new needed to be combined, the traditions adapted. That was the way forward. Without balance change could not occur. It wasn't only about mutual respect. It went far beyond that. It was respect for yourself. Only then could you give it to someone else. The land is the mother and we are her babies. He missed his mother. He regretted not knowing her. It had been beyond his control, though. He would find another mother. She could substitute for the thing he most needed. He had been seeking love through marriage but it hadn't worked. It would never work if he didn't learn how to give it first. First he needed to train himself. How was he going to do that? He could go to Doris; he could ask Doug. In the end, though, they could only help so much. It was up to him to make the real changes.

He didn't agree with the brutal punishment, but he didn't agree with the crime either. They were both vicious in their own ways. There were courts for that sort of thing. Which court was he in?

All the thoughts running through his head made him dizzy. After leaving the confines of the rock-hole, Billy had told Doug that he would catch up with him later. He said he needed time to think. Doug had joked that he'd better not take too long or his tea would get cold. Billy had laughed along with him but wasn't at all in a joking mood. He had wandered out of the crevice leading to the rockhole and moved along a ridge. He felt drained and found a spot to sit on a small hillock overlooking the town. He could see a line of mountains about fifty kilometres away. In his raised position he again had the impression that he was sitting on the edge of a river. A very wide river, with the ranges in the distance forming the opposite bank. It struck him how old the land was. How it must have changed over time. He stared at the ranges and the sun seemed to sit on top of them. It wouldn't be long before it set completely behind them. Involuntarily he shook, and a shiver ran down his spine. The air had cooled dramatically without the sun to keep it warm.

He looked down at his feet and spotted a digital wristwatch lying in the sand. Its display was blinking and apart from some weathering it appeared to be in perfect working order. The display read: 17:30 27-8-93. The time and date seemed insignificant now. The watch was just a piece of plastic and not really worth a thing. Nor was time for that matter. He stood up and threw it as far as he could. It clattered on the rocks below. One day in the future someone else would find it. As worthless as it was. In all probability it would still be working; or maybe the sun would have damage it beyond recognition. At any rate, it was of no consequence. Time was of no consequence. He felt released from its constraints. Even the land was timeless. Although it was ancient, it was new to him. The shackles had dropped. He was free.

Billy sensed that he had found his home. During the short time he had spent in the little community he had experienced things which both shocked and challenged him. For the first time in his life he didn't feel alone. He felt part of a family, with people who understood and supported him. He had found a purpose. He now had a history and a past, even though not all the history was personally his own.

Doug's words rang loud in his ears: 'The culture must not die.'

The culture, the lore, the history, and all the stories could not just be recorded and filed away. It had to live on in the people. It had to be exercised for it to remain healthy and grow in strength. It had to live in him and others if it was ever to survive. There was so much he didn't know, so much he still had to learn. His real education had just begun. Once he had mastered it to some degree he should take this knowledge and pass it on. There were no real mysteries or secrets; they were there for everyone. The only criterion was respect. Respect for what he had learned; that it was a gift, and in turn he could give this wonderful gift to others. It would take him some time to fully understand the nature of what he had received, but for now he knew that it was incredibly valuable. Not something physical; not material and to be selfishly harboured, like the possessions he had owned in the world he had recently left behind.

The land, the people and the law—all were tied together. One could not exist without the others. They were firmly linked, inseparable yet fragile. It was also up to him to protect, enforce and uphold them. He felt honoured that he had been allowed to become part of it. Not only that: it had also truly become part of him. He had something.

He thought back to the night at the roadhouse and his first meeting with Pidgin. His time had come; a door had opened for him that he never knew existed. It had set him on his present path, and for that he felt eternally thankful.

He sat and stared at the setting sun. It was glowing red on the horizon. The sky slowly changing from pink to purple. Doug had said it was the most hazardous time of the day. There were dangers out there and they could be approaching right now. Only now he had no fear. He had the strength and would bravely face whatever was to come.

Exhaustion suddenly swept over him. He gave in to it and let his body go limp. All apprehension melted away. He had some answers; not all of them, but it was a good start. He was relieved.

Pidgin stood silently behind Billy. His shadow stretched out in an infinite, long line behind him. It flowed out like an endless, great inland river. He lifted one hand from his club and lowered it towards Billy's shoulder. He squeezed it in a fatherly gesture. Pidgin's shadow swept forward. It enveloped Billy, who had one last glimpse of the setting sun before darkness engulfed the land. Then everything went black.

EPILOGUE

....

1843

My familiar has appeared to me in a dream. He has shown me a great many things. I saw my people torn apart and virtually disintegrated. An alien and incredibly advanced tribe will take over our land. They will drive us from it and in so doing also drive us from our way of life. Some of us will go willingly, enticed by the things they offer. They will come with demons which will carve up the earth. They will bring black rain which will destroy our country and make it infertile. They will move and remove the waters so that we can no longer survive through the dry times. Many of our totems will suffer and some will cease to exist. Maybe my own totem, Katararrtji, the spinifex pigeon, will be one of them. They will clear the land of all vegetation and introduce their own totems. This will stop the rains.

As our food and water supplies are eradicated we will come to depend on them for these things. They will take advantage of this and use us to help them destroy our own land. This will, in turn, break down our system of law and family. They will bring with them evil spirits which will take over our bodies and decimate us. Some of us will fight, but our weapons will be no match for theirs. They will take our women and water down our blood. Many of our kinsmen will lose their language, although some will be clever and will foster a new way with this new nation. Many of us will leave our homelands and never return, adopting their way of living. Those that do will give up our beliefs and system of law. Everyone will suffer because of this, the old and the new.

In the dream my familiar has also shown me hope. We will survive, although much will be lost. We will adapt as we always have. This land is in constant change and we have managed to adjust with it as time has passed. It is our way. We will do it again. Although with this great change it will take more than just a few seasons. The rain will come, as will the dry. This cycle will repeat a great many times before this transformation is over.

We will have to show the new custodians how to treat the land with respect. There will come a time when they are ready to learn from us. We must try to keep the lore alive until that time comes.

More than this, in my dream I saw yet another hope. I will have a descendent who no longer knows the old ways. He will be drawn to learn them. He will be one of few who will bridge the gap. The few will grow in number and become many. They will try to re-establish a new order. It will be difficult, as much will have transpired which can no longer be reversed.

I am fearful for the time that is to come. I am unsure how to tell my tribesmen about this dream. It is a new dream and they will be sceptical. I must try to find a way to warn them of the dangers to come. Although the future is clouded it is clear that a great change is coming and there will be very little we can do about it. It will sweep over us like a giant sand storm. Those who can hold their breath long enough will survive. Those who can't will perish. I see that, at the very least, hope lies within my own family. I will try to instil this hope in my offspring and teach them to hold onto our values. I will endeavour to do the same.

Perhaps, like my familiar, there is another way to warn them—to guide them—even once my physical body no longer walks this realm. I will consult my spiritual brothers for guidance. They will accept my dream. They will help. They always do. I will do all in my power to ensure that my sons and daughters find the right path, even though the future is so unclear. Together, we will be resilient and steadfastly uphold our values, law and culture.

ABOUT THE AUTHOR

P. J. Whittlesea is an author and singer-songwriter. Originally from Australia, he now resides in Amsterdam in The Netherlands. *Loreless* is his debut novel.

More information can be found about current and upcoming works at the author's website.

www.pjwhittlesea.com

Are you curious what happened to Billy?

Read the deleted chapter in the Companion.
Also includes: maps, timelines, research and
other insights.
Available as a digital download via:
www.pjwhittlesea.com/loreless-companion

CPSIA information can be obtained
at www.ICGtesting.com
Printed in the USA
LVHW041913030220
645677LV00006B/1126